Priority Books PUBLICATIONS

P.O. Box 2535
Florissant, MO 63033

Copyright ©2008 by Kareem Tomblin

All Rights reserved.No part of this book may be reproduced or transmitted in any forms by any means, electronic, mechanical, photocopy, recording or otherwise, without the consent of the Publisher, except as provided by USA copyright law.

Edited by:Lynel Johnson Washington (1st), Terrra Little (2nd)
Cover Designed by Karoz Norman back by MAJALUK
Typist: Annetta Pool
Manufactured in the United States of America
Library of Congress Control Number: 2008939348
ISBN 13: 978-0-9816483-6-1
ISBN 10: 0-9816483-6-3

For information regarding discounts for bulk purchases, please contact Prioritybooks Publications at 1-314-306-2972 or rosbeav03@yahoo.com.

You can contact the author at: Kareem Tomblin #10119-058, Federal Correction Center, Post Office Box 52020/Unit B-2, Bennettsville, SC 29512.

DEATH, NO EXCEPTIONS!
Somebody has got to pay........
by Kareem Abdul Tomblin

Published by Prioritybooks Publications
Missouri

DEATH, NO EXCEPTIONS!
Somebody has got to pay........
by Kareem Abdul Tomblin

ACKNOWLEDGEMENTS

First and foremost, I give thanks and praise to the Almighty God for blessing me to come forth from my mother's womb alive and well—with purpose—a purpose that only He in His divine wisdom and foresight knows the proper time and place for such purpose to unfold and be fulfilled. If I ever become anything of significance on this planet it will be because He has ordained it so. Thank You, Lord.

Special thanks to my dear mother, Geneva Tomblin-Jackson, for not aborting me, or giving up on me while I was lost out in the streets thuggin'! I love you, Momma. You will forever remain my # 1 lady!

Special thanks to my big sister, friend, and mentor, Rose Jackson-Beavers, for believing in a brother enough to give me an opportunity to express myself to the world through Prioritybooks Publications. Sister, your purpose is great on this earth. And you are definitely appreciated!

Thank you, Adeesha, for encouraging your mother to publish my work because you enjoyed reading my manuscript and thought it would not only appeal to the young, but had a valuable message of forgiveness.

Special thanks to: Dobbie Tomblin, Yolanda "Yo-Yo" Rogers, Eimmis, Minister Jerome Tomblin, Kendra, Ann Rogers, Yolanda "Happy" Alexander, Chera Goodwin, Kevin Goodwin, Katina, Lachandra "Boo" Beasley, Felicia Knox, Marshay Knox, Little Kareem, Annetta "Preaches," Nicole Robinson, Tracey Hubbard, Jennifer Daniels, Ms. Jackson, Dr. Smith, Shorty Faye, My big boo and most loyal friend, Sia Georgiou and Lil Stephanie, Ronald "Mo" Atwaine McKoy, Lamont Twitty, Eric Harnette, Johnny Gore, Adrian Ladson, Big Leroy, Adrian "AD" Davis, Donald "D-Nice" Thomas, Michael "Reddy Mike" Rozelle, Timothy "Worm," Christopher Thomas, Jersey, the author of *Crime'z N Passion!* And yo, the list goes on...Rob, you know I stay cuttin' your hair, boy! Leesa and Tiffany "Queen" Moore. Also, Jamie Graham, what up, knuckle head! Eddie Mungo, what up? "L.C." Special thanks to the Blackband Brotherhood Klan

(BBK):Big Reginald Potts, Riece, Lamont Lucas (Bilal, the poet), Big Jermaine Beckham, Damon Regan, Tony Caldwell, "PT," and Chris. Bruthas, the communities that we through ignorance help to destroy, we must now through godly wisdom and knowledge go back and rebuild. We can do it if we stay focused and for real about helping our people!

Also, to all of my incarcerated bruthas and sistahs, remember that the powers that be can indeed remove us from the outside world due to us breaking laws, and as a result of UNJUST LAWS. However, they cannot remove us from the plan and purpose that Almighty God has ordained for each and every one of us to fulfill! So don't ever throw in the towel, for your life is not over with. No, not by a long shot! Study while in prison, and do whatever else you need to do to better yourself, in an effort to SHOW to those who want to keep us behind steel doors and concrete walls that we can rise above thuggism and negativity if we change our minds to focus on the positive, as well as ACT on such!

Oh, yeah, to all of my critics who told me I couldn't, THANK YOU! I used your destructive criticism of me to do what I knew in my heart that I could do. Now stop hatin' and start congratulating!

Kareem Abdul Tomblin

DEDICATION

I humbly dedicate this book to my baby sister, Dobbie "Dee-Dee" Tomblin. Thank you, little sister, for your unconditional love and support of me over the years. When I was arrested and detained by the Feds, you were a little girl. Now, you are a full grown woman of substance. You inspire me. And when the Creator decides to bless me with a Queen, I hope she is as beautiful and loyal as you.

Also, I dedicate this book to my little cousin, Lynnette. I love you little cuz, keep your head up; the sky is the limit for you!

"Whatever decision one chooses to make in life, make such carefully, with 'wise' direction; Because in this world of sin—motivated by dividend$, one slip or wrong turn could lead to death, no exceptions!"

Back In The Day

CHAPTER ONE
Coke and Cash!

One Friday evening, in the Queen City of Charlotte, North Carolina, William Earl Holly was keeping a close watch on fly, thirty-two-year-old Monica Sparks. Yolanda Owens, a chick William occasionally dated, told him Monica was a single mother of a four-year-old son named Ali. And that she had been left a substantial amount of coke and cash by her late boyfriend and son's father, big Jay-Jay, who had gotten killed three months ago over a drug deal gone bad. William thought hard about this information after receiving it from Yolanda, who happened to be Monica's best friend and was dead drunk at the time she made it known to him. He figured if he could perhaps catch the high rollin' Monica Sparks slippin', he could score big, provided that everything Yolanda had said of her friend was actually true. Having only twenty-two dollars to his name, William decided that this was the day he'd find out. So, he waited patiently in the parking lot of the Johnson Daycare Center, where Monica picked up her son five days a week without fail. He did so with absolutely no accomplice. The last guy he took with him on a robbery of a jewelry shop that was owned and operated by Asians, got him caught six hours later by ratting him out to the authorities. William ultimately had to serve three years and eight months in a state prison for the robbery. When he was finally released four months ago, he vowed on everything he loved to never again return to prison alive. From now on, he decided he'd commit any future robberies solo.

******

William's wait was over, because just as he had expected from close observation of Monica, she pulled up at a quarter to six in her dark blue chromed-out Benz 190.

She stepped out, undoubtedly looking like a woman who could have very easily been mistaken for the twin sister of movie star actress, Halle

Berry. The only visible difference was Monica's butt. It was so big and sexy, Ray Charles in his blind state, could've seen it.

Monica was wearing nylon black, white, and red Air Jordan for Women sweats, along with matching Air Jordan Nike tennis shoes. As she endeavored to make her way inside the daycare center, William watched and shook his head at her fat booty bouncing in her nylon sweat pants. She had to be wearing a thong, William thought. Had he not been so focused on getting paid, he would have definitely whipped his penis out of his jeans and masturbated right there in his stolen Honda Accord. Instead, he fired up a Newport cigarette and waited a few more anxious minutes.

Finally, Monica exited the building carrying her son hugged up in her arms with his feet around her waist. Her son appeared to be sleeping. She approached the passenger side of her car to secure her son in the seat belt, totally unaware of the six-foot, slender, dark-skinned thug methodically making his way toward her.

William had his right hand inside the pocket of his all white hoody sweater, while his left one was being used to flick his cigarette onto the concrete of the parking lot. The closer he got to Monica, the harder his heart began to beat. He caught her lifting her head from being bent over inside the car. Through her peripheral vision, she spotted William behind her, but before being able to say or do anything, she felt a hard object being pressed into her side. It was a straight razor William had pulled from his hoody sweater. Monica perceived it to be a gun and froze in fear of being shot down in cold blood.

******

"Bitch, I'm only gonna say this once. Getcha ass in the car and do exactly as I say."

Monica clumsily walked around to the driver's side of her car and got in. When she got situated, she saw William placing her son onto his lap with the straight razor to his face. Thus, awakening Ali from his sleep.

"I promise you if you scream or do anything out of the ordinary, I'll cut his throat...do you understand me?" Uttered William, with his teeth clamped together and loud enough for her to get his message.

Monica gripped the steering wheel tightly. "Yes, I understand you...

"Alright then, dammit, get that key in that ignition and drive!"

Trembling like a homeless individual on a cold and frosty winter's night, coupled with seeing absolutely no one else in the parking lot of the daycare center to witness this horror, she did nothing short of what he demanded and drove off.

******

"I just want you to take me to where you're hiding the coke and cash... that's all I'm here for," William demanded.

"What coke and cash?" Monica replied.

"Look, dammit, I ain't here to play games with you. Now, I'm telling you, take me to where you're hiding the coke and cash!" Monica didn't say anything for a few seconds and her silence provoked him into becoming even more angry and aggressive.

"You think I'm bullshittin' wit' you?"

"Nooo, I don't think you're bullshittin..."

"Yes the fuck you do! But I'ma show yo' ass betta than I can tell ya!" William gripped her son's pinky finger and cut a significant portion of it off. Little Ali immediately screamed in pain. Blood gushed all over

William's all-white hoody sweater, but he didn't give a damn. He just grabbed the remaining part of Ali's pinky and squeezed it to minimize the flow of blood. Then he looked over at Monica, who found it hard to drive and listen to the screams of her son. "Now, what the fuck is up? You gon' be straight wit' me or not?"

She panicked and nearly ran a nearby stoplight. "Okay, okay, okay...the coke and cash are at my condo."

"How much is it?" William asked fiercely, wide-eyed with a wicked grin on his face. His facial expression was so mean looking that Monica thought he had to be a real live psycho.

"About three kilos of coke and seventy some thousand in cash. If you want more, a friend is gonna deliver more to me in the morning..."

Unwilling to wait for what wasn't already there, he ordered her to just drive straight to her condo, while at the same time throwing Ali's severed skin out of the window.

******

Upon arrival, Monica parked directly in front of her place. "This is where I live," she said.

"Does someone else live here with you?"

"No, only my son and I."

"Then why are your lights on?"

"I forgot to turn them off before I left, that's all. No one else is here."

"Well, me and your son are gonna remain here in the car while you go inside to get the coke and cash. But if you try anything, and I do mean anything, I'm killing your son. That's a muthafuckin' promise! You've got four minutes to be back out here. Four fuckin' minutes!"

Monica rushed out of the car. When she did, Ali started crying harder. William put his hand over Ali's mouth, just enough to muffle his cry without suffocating him. Monica went directly upstairs to where her stash was. She grabbed a pillowcase from her bed, opened her safe after two horrible tries and stuffed everything that looked like coke and cash into the pillowcase. She stormed back downstairs and out the door, opened the driver's side car door and handed the pillowcase to William.

"It's all there," said Monica, struggling to catch her breath.

"It sure as hell better be!" William replied.

He took a quick look inside the pillowcase and realized she was telling the truth. The pillowcase was filled with rolls of cash and Ziploc bags full of powder cocaine.

"Now leave me the keys to your car," he demanded. Monica handed them over.

He released Lil' Ali and backed out of her driveway, leaving her standing there looking dumbfounded and in a state of shock.

******

As William zoomed out of her neighborhood and out of sight, Monica hurried back inside her condo with Ali in her arms. She phoned 9-1-1 for the medics. She elected not to alert the cops concerning her Benz being stolen for fear of bringing heat onto herself, because unbeknownst to her robber, directly inside the glove compartment of her car were five ounces of crack and a .38 revolver. If only she could've gotten to her gun. Many thoughts raced through her head, like whether or not she had been set up. And if so, by whom? In any event, the one constant in the equation of her thinking was that, whoever this dude was who had done this to her and Lil Ali had picked the wrong chick to mess wit'! And by any means necessary, she would use all of her available resources to prove it.

Revenge: (v.)

"To impose injury in return for injury received."

CHAPTER TWO
It's On!

Yes, sirrrr, it's on now! William said to himself as he drove a few miles before deciding to ditch Monica's Benz. He knew beyond a shadow of a doubt, that he had hit the jackpot wit' this lick, and he could hardly contain his composure. But at the same time, his jubilation was briefly disturbed as he contemplated the fact that he'd had to cut a child's finger to get what he'd gotten. The thought of such angered him, causing him to hit the steering wheel wit' his fist. "Damn, that's a stupid ass, red bitch," he said inside her car to himself. "She would rather protect this shit—looking down at the pillowcase full of coke and cash—than the life and limb of her own fuckin' child! He flirted with the thought momentarily, before completely letting it go.

"Fuck it. What's done is done!" he said, while pulling halfway into a booth at a nearby carwash, where he grabbed the pillowcase and bailed out. He headed straight across the street, speed walking wit' absolutely no time to waste, to a payphone in the parking lot of a McDonald's, with the express intent of calling his friend Emily Parker.

******

Emily Parker was a twenty-nine-year-old, beautiful, intelligent, white chick. She was down for whatever, like a street soldier! She believed that, IF IT DIDN'T MAKE DOLLAR$, IT DIDN'T MAKE SENSE. William had met her while he was in state prison, through his roommate, Timothy Sinclair, who was also from Charlotte, North Carolina. Emily and Timothy's girl worked together at the Foot Locker in Southpark Mall and were very close. They would both come up together and visit him and Timothy. Sometimes they would even bring the two of them balloons packed wit' weed, for William and Timothy to get their hustle on.

William felt Emily was the only one he could trust to come scoop him

DEATH, NO EXCEPTIONS!

up. So, he phoned her crib.

"Hello, Emily speaking."

"Emily, this is William. Listen, I'm about seven miles from where you live. I'm at the McDonald's right off the interstate. I need you to come get me."

"Come get you? Boy, I'm 'bout to get in the bathtub," she replied.

"Look, damn that! This is an emergency. Delay that bath and come get me before they do."

"They who?" she asked before hearing absolute silence and then the dial tone after he hung up. But just as he knew she would, she pulled up fifteen minutes later in her all black Nissan Pathfinder wit' the midnight factory tint on the windows. Relieved to see her like a pregnant woman was relieved of the unbearable pains of giving birth to a newborn, he jumped into the backseat of the Pathfinder, immediately taking notice of the sexy blonde chick sitting up front with her.

******

Emily noticed the pillowcase William was trying to cuff under his right arm, as well as the very visible blood stains on his all white Timberland hoody, and voiced her concern. "You called me like a gang of muthafuckahs were after you; had me worried like hell!"

"That's exactly what I thought it was about to be," said William, stationing himself in the backseat while she slowly pulled off. "I got into a little confrontation that turned violent, fuckin' over a dice game, which involved a lot of loop. Shit. Had to punch a nigga in his face! I believe I broke the muthafuckah's nose...fuckin' got blood all over my damn new hoody!"

Such was all that he knew to tell her to cover up the truth of what had really gone down. She looked back at him through her rearview mirror.

"You alright though, right?"

"I am now," he said, taking a deep breath and still checking out the blonde up front. His number one weakness had always been females.

Emily introduced the blonde. "This is my cousin, Rachael. She's down here visiting for the weekend from Savannah, Georgia."

William leaned a little closer to catch a clearer view of Rachel as she turned in his direction, all shy-like.

"Okay. Hiya doin', Miss Rachael?" he said flirtatiously.

"Pretty good. Nice to meet you," she replied in a voice that would make a one-hundred-year-old, impotent man's penis stand erect.

"Nice to meet you, too," he said.

"So where you trying to go?" asked Emily.

"Your place will be fine. Hell, it's closer. I need to get cleaned up anyways."

******

As they cruised to Emily's place, she turned up the volume on her Dr. Dre's Chronic CD and pointed out to Rachael certain spots in the city where everybody she knew hung out. While they chatted about this spot and that spot, William took a look inside the pillowcase and took out one of the Ziploc bags full of coke to taste it. The coke instantly numbed the very tip of his tongue, thereby letting him know for certain that he had gotten his hands on some good product. Emily was the perfect person to help him get rid of it, because she knew damn near every hustler in Queen City. He closed the Ziploc bag back up, laid his head back on the seat and contemplated his next move.

He planned to drop a nice amount of cash off to his Auntie Annie Pearl, who had raised him since he was just a baby. His biological mother, Annie Pearl's youngest sister, was a heroin addict and too addicted to take good care of him. After his mother had him, he was told that she put William straight in Annie Pearl's hands and was never seen again. His father's identity was also a mystery to him. But his Auntie Annie Pearl was not the type to put him up for adoption, or have him placed in some foster home to be mistreated by strangers. She was his blood relative, so she took him in. If he wasn't gonna look out for anyone else at this moment of having money in his pocket, he was gonna look out for her.

Then there was his homie and ex-cellmate, Timothy, who had hooked him up wit' Emily while in prison. On the day he left prison, William promised Timothy that once he got on his feet, he would no doubt look out for him by making sure that he kept some money in his account, so that Timothy could buy whatever he needed from the prison commissary. It was a promise he felt he had to keep.

Emily's jeep came to a halt and William's thoughts were interrupted as she shouted over the Dr. Dre CD. "We're here!"

CHAPTER THREE
I Got Jacked!

Medics arrived at Monica's condo. The sight of the bright red, orange, and white lights from the ambulance were enough to attract spectators from her predominately black and white middle class, quiet, nothing-out-of-the-ordinary-going-on type of neighborhood. Her neighbors rarely saw anything that peaked their curiosity and stirred up gossip. Today, however, they found themselves peeking out of their windows, standing in their doorways and on their little porches, whispering to one another as to what the problem could be. Then, suddenly, they all saw the medics bringing Monica's son, Ali, out wit' his left hand heavily wrapped and bandaged, and Monica following closely behind. She informed the medics that, while playing, Ali had accidentally cut his finger off wit' the kitchen knife that she mistakenly left on her bedroom floor in a Domino's Pizza box.

As she stepped into the back of the ambulance, one of her neighbors, Mrs. Rose, a retired high school teacher, whom Monica talked wit' regularly and attended church wit' almost every Sunday, approached the ambulance, walking slowly and leaning on her cane. "Ah, honey, is everythang awe-right?"

"Yes, m'am, Mrs. Rose. Everything is fine," Monica said, looking down on Mrs. Rose from the back of the ambulance. "My son just had a little accident and cut his finger. We're on our way now to the hospital to have the doctor take a look at it," she said, hating wit' a passion having to lie to the woman who had always treated her like a daughter.

"Well, call me later," said Mrs. Rose.

"Yes, m'am. I sure will."

Mrs. Rose turned and walked back toward her condo. She could sense in her spirit that Monica was withholding the truth from her. Mrs. Rose wasn't a stupid woman. She had been around for awhile; seventy-three years to be exact. Her third-eye told her that Monica's face and overall demeanor were too distraught for her to not have undergone some type of trouble. But rather than be nosy, Mrs. Rose entered her condo, dropped straight to her knees in front of her favorite rockin' chair, and uttered a prayer for Monica and Lil Ali.

******

On the way to the hospital, Monica called Ricky Blakely from her cell phone. As she waited on him to answer his phone she thought about the first time she met him.

Ricky was a twenty-eight-year-old, light brown skinned associate of Monica's, whom people would often walk up to and tell him that, without his corn roll braids, he looked just like Suge Knight, the legendary owner of Death Row Records. Monica considered him a brother and true friend. But many in the streets feared him, because he was six-feet-seven and weighed 280 pounds, solid. He was the type who loved to fight, and no one who knew of him in the streets dared to contest him in a head up, one-on-one fistfight. Ricky could knock your ass slam out with one punch, with his big, heavy hands. Ricky's hands were what Monica always remembered most about him, after their first introduction. Monica was introduced to Ricky through her son's father and her sweetheart, Big Jay-Jay, a year before his demise. Ricky had come over to her and Jay-Jay's condo one Saturday morning to deliver a package to Jay-Jay. Ricky and Jay-Jay were sitting around the seven-chair dining table in the kitchen when Jay-Jay called her to the kitchen.

"Yo, Monica, sweetheart, come here a minute," he yelled.

When Monica arrived, Jay-Jay handed her two large, medium-brown paper bags. Monica knew exactly what those bags contained, because Jay-Jay, on a weekly basis, would hand over to her either brown paper bags like the ones she was now in possession of, or large, clear Ziploc bags. The bags were always full of thousands of dollars worth of pot.

Monica took the bags and was about to head upstairs to place them where she always placed large sums of pot—in her safe in the bedroom. But Jay-Jay stopped her and said, "And oh yeah, Monica, this is Ricky, an associate of mine. If ever he come over here with my permission and give you something for me, take it. He's not the police, he's good people."

Monica thought to herself that Ricky had to be good people without Jay-Jay even making mention of that, because Jay-Jay never allowed any of his associates who dealt drugs to come to his home, where he, his woman and his child laid their heads.

Ricky was truly the first and Monica dared not question the wisdom of Jay-Jay doing so. One thing she understood was her place, and that sometimes hustlers did what they felt needed to be done. Jay was a hustler and he had been hitting Ricky off with a kilo and a half every other week for the price of $30,000 - $20,000 for a whole kilo and $10,000 for half of one. Jay-Jay never once had trouble about his money being straight when it came from Ricky. Ricky was so straight up and on time with Jay-Jay's money that many times Jay-Jay wouldn't even count it. He was a man Jay-Jay undeniably found trustworthy enough to come under his roof. After he introduced Monica to Ricky, Jay-Jay looked over at Ricky and said, "Ricky, man, this is my sweetheart and queen, Monica. She's the mother of our son, Ali."

"Nice to meet you, Monica," said Ricky.

"You, too," replied Monica.

"Now Ricky, show Monica your hands for a second," Jay-Jay requested.

Ricky wasn't sure why, but he figured Jay-Jay had his reasons. So he held both hands out for Monica to view. He turned them over so she could check out both sides.

"You see how big brutha's hands are?" Jay-Jay asked.

It took Monica no time at all to answer him. Hell, Stevie Wonder could've seen how big Ricky's hands were. In addition, Monica noticed how rough they looked, like they had been used to punch concrete walls. "Hmmm, hmmm," Monica responded,

"They are big. Now, why you ask?"

"Because, if I ever hear about you giving my good loving away to any busta ass sucker in this city, guess what's gonna happen to such a person?"

Monica sucked her teeth and put her hand on her hip. "What's gonna happen, Jay?"

"He gon' get knocked the fuck out by those hands. Ain't that right, Ricky?"

"You know I' aint got no problem doing it, dawg," replied Ricky.

"Whatever, Jay. I know your elevator don't go all the way up, so I ain't even gonna entertain that thought. Anyway, again, nice to meet you, Ricky."

After Big Jay-Jay's demise, it was Ricky who consoled Monica with the embracement and words of assurance that whatever she needed of and from him, she could get at her beckoning.

Monica also received much consoling from her childhood friend, Yolanda, whom Monica had hooked Ricky up with.

Monica knew from having already met Ricky and dealing with him while Jay-Jay was alive, that Ricky's consoling and embracement was genuine. Coupled with the fact that after they had started making money together, no matter where they would be together—whether in a club partying or in a mall shopping—Ricky never let anyone get too close to her without first having to go through not only him, but also his number one ace, Bootsy O'Shay.

The moment Monica met Bootsy through Ricky and Yolanda, she instantly discerned that Bootsy was of the same genuine spirit as Ricky. The only difference was, Bootsy wasn't getting his knuckles bruised from fist fighting anyone. He was doing nothing short of putting hot lead in the fanny of anyone who dared to violate him or his clique of Ricky, Monica, and Yolanda.

He, Ricky, and Yolanda had met late one night at the Jaguar Club off Independence Blvd. At the time, Bootsy knew neither one of them. But while Ricky was on his way to his milky-white Cadillac Seville, accompanied by Yolanda, he dropped a bundle of money that was being held together by a rubber band. Bootsy went to retrieve it. He then walked over to Ricky, who was sitting in his car and said, "Yo, bruh, you dropped this?"

Ricky looked at him and then patted his pockets. He wanted to make sure that the cash Bootsy was handing to him was in fact his. Sure enough, it was.

"Grab that for me, Yolanda, before I fuckin' lose it again." Yolanda grabbed the money.

Ricky then said, "Now give young blood a grand out of that."

When Bootsy heard him tell her that, he interjected, "Naw, man, you don't have to do that."

"Yes, I do. Now, please take the money for your honesty, cause I don't know too many people who would have given me my money back. That's nearly five grand in that stack."

Bootsy still didn't take it. "Look, young blood, I'm giving you this as a show of my appreciation. Plus, you look like a brutha who might be doing a little something." (Ricky was talking about hustling.) "I might be able to take you to another level with that."

Ricky could see that Bootsy was clean-cut, with a tight fade and waves going to the side. He was dressed pretty nicely in his USED by ELI blue jean Khaki shirt that was unbuttoned at the neck, enough for Ricky to see the two thick diamond-cut gold rope chains he was wearing. One chain had a 9mm gold medallion. The other, praying hands. Bootsy's baggy jeans hung down at his buttocks, heavily drooping over his black suede and leather Baileys. Ricky also noticed that Bootsy was dark skinned, five-feet-eleven and about 165 pounds.

"I do a little something-something. Nothing major, though," Bootsy said.

"How 'bout hopping into the backseat?" requested Ricky.

Bootsy hopped in.

"That little something you talking 'bout is hustling coke, right?"

Bootsy cracked a smile and muttered, "Naw, bruh. I put pistols to niggas' heads and make 'em give it up."

Bootsy placed his hand on the butt of the 9mm at his waist. Yolanda watched him do it. She didn't say anything though. She figured if he was out to rob them, he never would have given Ricky his money back.

Ricky was looking at him in the rearview mirror. But after Bootsy indicated that he was a stick-up kid, Ricky turned around with the quickness and said, "You do what?"

"I rob, well, let me change that, I TAKE from arrogant, drug dealing muthafuckahs who think they all that!"

Ricky didn't like robbing folks at all. He thought robbing others was a dirty business, which required too much violence and looking over your shoulders for those who would retaliate. "Young blood, not to knock your hustle, but it's too much money out here to make doing other things than to be involved with that type of shit."

Bootsy thought before responding. He didn't want to offend anyone. "One thing is for sure, Ricky, I would never consider robbing a guy like you, man."

"How you know my name?" asked Ricky.

"I heard the bartender mention it when you was at the bar and you yelled, *All drinks on me*. I downed two drinks that you paid for and thought to myself, that's a good dude right there. You know real recognizes real..."

Ricky looked at Yolanda, who was nodding her head up and down slowly, indicating that she was feeling Bootsy was an alright guy. Ricky then said, "Yolanda, give young blood that whole damn stack." Yolanda tossed the money into Bootsy's lap. This time he didn't refuse. Again, he didn't want to offend anyone.

"By the way," said Ricky, "since you already know my name, this is my crazy ass friend, Yolanda." Yolanda hit Ricky hard on his shoulder with her fist. "Don't be telling him I'm crazy."

Ricky smirked. "Just playing girl," he responded.

Yolanda then looked at Bootsy and introduced herself. "What's up? I'm Yolanda."

Yolanda was a shorty. Five-foot-four, to be exact, with beautiful black skin. She looked as if she were originally from Ethiopia. Her hair was in a French wrap. Her nose was small and pointy, with a small diamond earring in it. Yolanda's eyes were as dark as her skin and her cherry red, painted lips were thin and sexy. She was wearing a cherry red, skintight skirt that clearly revealed her nice ass and semi-thick thighs. Her red stiletto heels matched her skirt. To Bootsy she was a sexy ass chick, with a hood-like swagger.

"I'm Bootsy," he greeted, holding his hand out, which Yolanda shook first, followed by Ricky. "It's nice meeting the two of you."

From that moment on, whenever you saw Ricky, you saw Bootsy. And Ricky made sure that Bootsy never had to stick up anyone again for cash. Through Monica, Ricky and Bootsy were supplied with enough coke to keep both of their pockets fatter than fat. It would be these two street soldiers that Monica would not only alert, but rely on in aid of seeking vengeance.

*****

As Monica thought about that first meeting she waited anxiously for Ricky to answer his phone while she was in the back of the ambulance with little Ali. His phone rang seven times before he answered it knocking her out of her daydream.

Ricky answered his cell phone. "Yo, what's up?"

"What up, bruh? This Monica."

"I know. What's goin' on, sis? Been tryin' to reach you since earlier this evening," he said wit' slight frustration in his voice.

"Yeah, I got your page. Something bad has happened." She lowered her voice to damn near a whisper.

"I got jacked in the parking lot of the daycare center while picking up Ali. Nigga had me take him to my condo and everything. He got the coke and all my cash out the safe. Nigga even took my damn Benz!"

"Ah, fuck! Where are you?"

"I'm in the back of the ambulance."

"AMBULANCE?" he shouted. "Did the nigga hurt you?"

"No, he didn't touch me. He touched Ali!"

"What?" he shouted again in disbelief and anger.

"Yeah, and I'll tell you more later. Just meet me in about two hours at my condo."

"Bet," said Ricky before hanging up the phone. Then he looked toward Bootsy wit' one of the most ferocious demeanors Bootsy had ever seen him express.

"Monica got robbed earlier, bruh, and she wants us over at her crib in about two hours. Man, somebody gon' get fucked up for this one!" he said, poppin' his knuckles.

"Oh, fo' sho, my nigga!" said Bootsy, looking directly into Ricky's eyes, wit' his right hand on the 9mm glock that never left his waist, except for when it was time to put in work; something he didn't mind doing, especially for Monica.

CHAPTER FOUR
Emily's Apartment!

Meanwhile, at Emily's apartment, William was just stepping into the shower. He was determined to chill out for the rest of the night at her place. He had an extra pair of jeans and a dark green Polo shirt that he left at her place a month ago, when he last stayed the night there. However, what he didn't have was a clean pair of boxers. Wit' Emily knowing this, she looked over at Rachael in the living room and decided she was gonna tease him a bit.

"Aye, Will..." she shouted, winking her eye at Rachael and grinning.

"You want a pair of my panties to put on when you finish taking your shower?"

"Huh?" he said loudly, barely hearing her over the stereo he was listening to.

I said: "Do you want to put on a pair of my panties when you come out of the shower?"

Rachael shook her head, indicating to Emily that she was as crazy and wild as they came.

"Yeah, bring 'em to me," William replied. "Just make sure that they're large enough to hold all of this dick of mine!"

Rachael put both of her hands to her mouth in awe of hearing him talk like that.

The mention of his penis was more than enough to get Emily's kitty dripping, because she knew that if this brother wasn't packing anything else, he was packing a penis. So she proceeded in the direction of the bathroom door and entered. His body was fully covered wit' the Dove soap that she bathed wit' on a daily basis, and his enormous, black elephant trunk of a penis, which she loved so much was semi-erect and swinging from left to right between his legs. She continued to tease him for her own personal pleasure and gratification.

"What was that you said, Will?" she asked, standing there in his presence wit' one hand on her hips and the other being used to twirl a pair of her thongs around her finger.

"Emily, quit playin' wit' me. Now come here," he demanded of her. She took a few more steps closer to him, still twirling those thongs of hers on her finger. Once she was within arm's length of him, he grabbed a hold of her by the back of her head and pulled her all the way to him. As he did so, he snatched the thongs from her hand and threw them onto the bathroom floor. Then he directed her head toward his semi-erect penis. She started suckin' it without delay, like a hungry newborn suckin' a bottle full of Similac.

Damn, Emily still got the best oral sex in the whole Queen City, he thought as he enjoyed every single minute of it! So much so, that he found himself helpless to resist the temptation of sexing her freaky, horny self right there in the tub while showering!

His penis now fully erect, he lifted her head from it and told her to join him in the shower.

Wanting every bit of what she had just released from her mouth to deeply penetrate her hot, soaking wet kitty, she undressed as if completely under a spell and hopped inside the tub wit' him. He didn't hesitate in making her turn around, slightly bent over, wit' her hands up against the shower wall as if preparing to be shook down. Then he eased himself up to her and thrust his penis inside her kitty from the back, pushing every inch of it inside her, just like she liked it.

Curious as to what was taking her cousin so long to come back into the living room, Rachael decided to walk to Emily's bedroom, whereby she had to pass the bathroom. As she made her way to Emily's bedroom, she clearly heard the sounds of moaning and groaning, so she stopped at the bathroom door and peeked inside, hoping to go undetected. To her surprise, she saw William deep stroking her cousin from the back. Every expression on Emily's face as far as Rachael could see, bore witness to the euphoria of pleasure that she was experiencing from every stroke that he was sticking to her! Rachael decided to keep it moving, but before she stepped away from the door she saw William whip his penis out and nut all over her cousin's butt cheeks. That was the first time she'd ever seen a black man's penis up close and personal, and to her it was a penis to behold. One she was determined to have before traveling back home to Savannah, Georgia. However, for William, this sex encounter, although not planned by himself, but rather a product of Emily's own freakiness, suited him just fine. He felt he needed it to mellow him down from the intense excitement of having pulled off one of the biggest robberies he had ever conducted.

******

CHAPTER FIVE
Counting Money!

Having practically sexed the freak out of Emily, William stepped out of the shower, dried himself off and prepared to get dressed in Emily's bedroom, leaving her in the tub to clean herself up.

After getting dressed, he immediately grabbed his pillowcase from her closet, laid it on her bed and started counting money. He counted five geez off top, and put it to the side, along wit' another $1,200.

When Emily finally emerged from the shower, wit' only her towel wrapped around her from her breasts down to her butt, barely covering her visibly exposed clean shaven kitty, she noticed nothing but cash all over her bed. This stopped her in her tracks. But before she could utter a word, William tossed her a roll.

"That's five grand for you to do whatever you wanna do wit' it. I told you when I was in prison that I was gonna look out for you when I got straight, didn't I?" he said.

"Yeah, you did tell me that," she replied.

"Alright then, whatcha standing there looking all shocked for? And here's another $1,200. Do me a favor and send it to Timothy for me. You already know his address. Do dat as soon as possible. That five grand I just tossed you ain't nothing. You got more comin' as soon as we get rid of this coke."

"What coke?" she asked.

He pulled out the Ziploc bags full of powder cocaine and threw them on her bed. "This coke," he said.

"Three fuckin' keys of it! Now, getcha clothes on, roll us a blunt, and

DEATH, NO EXCEPTIONS!

call your cousin Rachael in here."

She called Rachael, but told William to hide the coke from her sight. He hid it, and as Rachael came into the room, he reached his hand out to her wit' some folded bill$ in between his fingers. She looked over at Emily, unsure of what to do. Emily nodded her head. "Take it," Emily said. "It's cool."

Rachael took the money from his hands and discovered that there were seven, one hundred dollar bills. She couldn't believe he would be kind enough to do something like this. No stranger had ever given her that much money. Wanting to tell him thank you, she looked over in his direction, but he, as if reading her thoughts, interjected, "Don't worry 'bout saying thank you, just know that whoever is cool wit' your cousin, is undoubtedly cool wit' me."

******

CHAPTER SIX
Carolina Medical Center

Monica was outside of the emergency room of Carolina Medical Center when Doctor Felix Hernandez, a Cuban immigrant who specialized in hand, wrist, ankle and foot surgeries, approached her. He found Monica conversing with a guy whose wife had a slight heart attack earlier that day while at work. Although not doing so well herself, Monica tried comforting the guy before excusing herself to speak with the doctor.

"Ah, Miss Sparks?" said Dr. Hernandez.

"Yes, that's me."

"I was informed that your son accidentally cut off his finger playing. Is that correct?" he asked, peeking through the tiny reading glasses sitting on the bridge of his nose and gripping his clipboard.

"That's correct, sir," she answered.

"We have stitched up the open flesh on his finger and he's doing fine. However, I was wondering if you happened to recover all the remaining parts of his severed finger?"

"No, I was in such a rush to get him to the hospital that it never once crossed my mind to recover it," she lied, hoping that there would be no more questions on the matter.

"Alrighty then, Miss Sparks. If you do happen to come across it, please do not hesitate to give me a call. There may be a strong possibility that we can reattach it, depending on the condition it's in. You can reach me here at extension 207. Your son will be free to go in a few more minutes, but he's going to be a bit tired from the anesthesia."

"Thank you very much, Doc."

"No problem," replied Dr. Hernandez as he headed back inside the emergency room.

******

While waiting on medical personnel to release her son, Monica called her mother to see if it would be alright for her to bring Ali over to her house to stay for the weekend. Her mother answered after four rings.

"Hello."

"Hello, Momma. This is Monica."

"Hey, baby. Hya doing?"

"I'm okay, Momma. I'm over here at Carolina Medical. Me and Ali. He had a little accident."

"Oh, is he alright?"

"He's fine, Momma. I'm on my way home. I was calling to see if I could drop him off over there for the weekend, because I've got a lot of cleaning to do around the house."

"Bring my baby on over, and grab me a can of Railroad Mill Snuff from the store on your way," requested her mother.

"Okay, Ma. See ya when we get there."

******

It was nearly 11:00 p.m. when Monica got to her mother's house wit' Ali. He was very sleepy, but awake enough to hold a brief conversation. Monica got down on her knees in her mother's living room to look Ali in his face, which resembled Big Jay-Jay, wit' his light brown skin and hazel green eyes.

She palmed his little chubby cheeks and kissed him on his lips.

"Mommy loves you very much, Ali. Okay?" Little Ali nodded his head.

"I don't want you to worry about anything. What happened today was an accident," she lied.

"Ma, that man today was very mean to me. What did I do for him to hurt my finger?" asked Ali, frowning.

Monica hugged him wit' tears mounting in her eyes. "You didn't do anything, baby. It was all an accident, that's all."

"But he screamed at you too, Ma, and put a knife at my throat."

"I know. That guy was just having a bad day. He's not gonna ever be mean to you or me ever again. Okay?"

"Yes, ma'am."

"I want you to get you some sleep and be nice to Grandma. When I come and get you Sunday, we're gonna go eat ice cream. Okay?"

"Okay."

"Monica, that cab driver is out there blowin' his horn for you," shouted her mother from her bedroom.

"I'm on my way right now." She kissed Ali one last time before sending him off to his grandmother's room.

"Ma, I'll call you later," Monica said, heading out the door and straight into the taxi. She was on her way back to her condo. But due to her stomach feeling emptier than a wagon making a lot of noise, she instructed the driver to go through the McDonald's drive-thru for a bite to eat.

******

As they tarried in the drive-thru, Monica noticed in plain view, right across the street, what looked like her Benz. *Naw, it couldn't be,* she thought to herself, but hopped out of the taxi momentarily to make sure. Upon closer scrutiny she discovered that it had to be hers. For no one in the Queen City of Charlotte, North Carolina had a chromed-out Benz 190 like hers.

She hopped back into the taxi.

"What a fuckin' coincidence," she shouted.

The driver looked at her through his rearview mirror.

"You say anything, miss?"

"Aw, yeah, forget this food. Drive me across the street to the carwash. I need to take a look at something."

"Sure," the driver replied.

They rolled across the street to the carwash, whereby she got out and walked right over to her Benz.

"I'll be damned," she said to herself, looking into her car and seeing her keys still in the ignition and everything else therein untouched, including the five ounces of cooked coke and the .38 revolver that was hidden in the glove compartment. The only discouraging sight inside her car was the blood she saw from her son's finger on the passenger seat. She tried cleaning it up with a towel she found in the backseat.

She then quickly hopped out of the car and walked back to the taxi.

"Sir, can you tell me how much I owe you?"

"$34.61 will about do it," replied the driver, after looking at the meter.

"No problem at all. But check this out, if I gave you $250.00 just to follow me to my place, would you do it?"

"Sure I would. Just tell me how far."

"Not far at all. Just tail me closely," said Monica, rushing back to her Benz.

******

When Monica arrived at her condo, Ricky Blakely and Bootsy O'Shay were there awaiting her arrival in Ricky's milky white Cadillac Seville.

As she pulled in alongside them, Ricky stepped out of his car, and so did Bootsy. Monica knew beyond a shadow of a doubt that both of them were strapped and ready for war by the way they were holding their hands in the pockets of their jackets. She immediately warned them not to look too suspicious, because her neighbors were the type that would call the police at the hint of the slightest glimpse of something looking out of the ordinary. Surely, two hardcore thug-looking black bruthas wit' their hands in their jackets would fit that description. Monica stepped out of her car.

"Ricky, you see that taxi driver behind me?" Monica asked.

"Yeah," he replied.

"Do me a favor and give him $250.00. He did me a big favor."

Death, No Exceptions!

Without questioning her request, Ricky walked to the taxi, dug into the right pocket of his jeans and pulled out a knot of nothing but hundred dollar bills. He took out three fresh one hundred dollar bills and handed them to the driver.

"Thanks for what you did for my sistah. We appreciate it."

"No problem at all," he replied, before backing out. Monica focused her attention on the driver, and gave him the thumbs up. He honked his horn and headed off into the night. Then Monica handed the five ounces of crack cocaine and her .38 revolver to Bootsy while she unlocked the door to her condo for them to enter.

******

"Did you get a good look at the muthafucka' who robbed you, Monica?" asked Ricky, unable to wait for her to initiate talking about it.

"Hell, yeah, I got a good look at that nigga! He was tall and dark-skinned wit' a real low haircut, almost bald-like. Yo, I don't know how that nigga crept up on me as silently as he did. All I know is, before I was able to look up, there he was, wit' a fuckin' straight razor at my back. You know the type of razor those barbers be using. Shit, I thought it was a gun though, so I let the nigga have his way. He knew about the coke and the money I had and all that. I know somebody had to hip him to me, bruh, because I don't mingle around the city like that."

Bootsy looked at her and shook his head, while taking a seat on the sofa, wit' the cocaine and her .38 revolver still in his hands.

"Well, we're gonna find out who this perpetrator is," said Ricky. "Bootsy and I have already been calling around the city. I got niggas off West Boulevard, North Charlotte, Grier Town, and niggas off West Trade and 5th Street wit' their ears and eyes open for any nigga comin' through selling weight, or even making mention of robbin' a female. The word is out and I trust that it's just a matter of time before something surfaces, because Charlotte ain't that big. Other than that, sis, Yolanda is flying in from New York in the morning. Me and Bootsy gon' scoop her up from the airport. And oh yeah, the reason I was paging you so hard earlier was because Yolanda left some money for me to give you. If I'm not mistaken, it's like $16,000. Plus, I got a little over $7,000 for you myself."

"I'll worry 'bout getting all of that tomorrow," said Monica. "Right now, I got this nigga on my mind. That black bastard didn't just rob me; he cut off my son's pinky finger!"

"Damn! Ricky didn't tell me that," Bootsy said to himself, while watching Monica pace up and down her living room floor. Ricky brought her pacing to a halt by placing his hands on her shoulders. Her pacing was causing Ricky to worry about her mental state.

"Look, sis, chill. Alright? We gon' handle it. Don't worry about that. I promise," stated Ricky, insistently.

Bootsy interjected. "Yo, whatcha want me to do wit' these five ounces of coke, Monica?"

"Just...just get rid of it, Bootsy! Okay? Just get rid of the shit!" she shouted, before storming upstairs.

Ricky and Bootsy both looked at each other and shrugged their shoulders.

"It is what it is, dawg," said Bootsy. "Just let her be for now."

******

(LATER ON: 2:37 a.m.)

Monica was upstairs, fast asleep in her bedroom, when she experienced the most unusual dream. In her dream, Big Jay-Jay appeared to her, dressed in all white, and sat right next to her on the edge of the queen-sized bed he paid for years ago. He gently placed her hand in his and began caressing it, just as he used to do when the two of them were together intimately.

"Monica, sweetheart," he said, "I love you. I always have and I always will, in spirit. You gave me our only child, a son, at a time in your life when you could have very easily said, 'Let's go to the clinic.' In those days, both of us had other things going on in our lives. You were in college, trying to pursue your degree in Business Administration, and I, of course, was on my grind out in the streets, clockin' dollars the only way I knew how."

"Nonetheless, we loved each other and we made it work, even in the face of your mom and dad hating my guts, because of my street endeavors. But Monica, I really never intended for you to be a part of my mess. I just didn't have enough time. The night I was shot, sweetheart, I never saw it coming. It all happened so fast. All I remember experiencing was my spirit ascending out of my body and seeing my earthly corpse lying in a pool of blood. I knew that my life on earth was officially over at that moment. I was experiencing death, no exceptions. I have been watching over you and Ali ever since. It's true that the dead can see everything, but there are certain events that we are unable to stop from occurring, like what you and our son experienced yesterday. Yet the dead are permitted to give advice and words of warning, which is why I am making this appearance in your dream. I want you to go back to pursuing your degree and exit the so-called 'Game' as soon as possible. If you elect to remain therein, I can assure you that it will take you places you are certainly not prepared to go."

Big Jay-Jay released her hand and disappeared. Monica sat up in her bed and looked all around the room, but saw no one. She still heavily sensed Big Jay-Jay's presence all around her. She grabbed his picture from the nightstand and looked at it, wit' tears flowing down her face like a river emptying itself after a heavy rain. Then she hugged it tightly, laid back down wit' the picture still in her arms, and thought about how much she really missed him. She was also contemplating taking his advice after all that she had in mind to do was over.

******

CHAPTER SEVEN
(Saturday, 9:23 a.m.)

Ricky, Bootsy and Yolanda were on the highway, coming from Douglas Airport. Ricky wasted no time informing Yolanda about what happened to Monica. The news came as a shock to her, and all she could do at the moment was bite down hard on her lip and clinch her fist in hopes of restraining the anger that was quickly surfacing within her.

"Yo, Ricky," said Yolanda, "forget about taking me to my crib. Let's go see Monica."

"Bet, but first I gotta stop by my spot and get something, which won't take but a hot minute," he replied.

****

Upon entering Monica's driveway, Ricky called her from his car phone.

She answered, "Yeah?"

"Monica, me, Bootsy, and Yolanda are out here in your driveway. Come open your door for us."

"Ummmm, what time is it?" asked Monica.

Ricky looked at the clock on the dashboard of his car.

"It's a little after ten."

"I'm on my way down. Give me a second."

Monica got out of bed. She was only wearing a waist-length T-shirt and a black fishnet G-string. She put Big Jay-Jay's picture back on the

Death, No Exceptions!

nightstand and grabbed her robe, then headed downstairs barefoot. Upon opening the door, she was warmly greeted by them all, especially Yolanda. She hugged Monica so tightly and for so long that Monica suspected either Ricky or Bootsy had already given her the heads-up on the robbery she had experienced.

As they embraced for what seemed like an eternity to Monica, Ricky went into the kitchen to fix himself some breakfast. Meanwhile, Bootsy removed his black leather, quarter-length coat, plainly exposing the butt of the 9mm glock tucked at his waist, and took a seat on Monica's sofa.

******

"Just getting up out of that bed, huh, girl? said Yolanda.

"Yeah. Hell, I had a long ass night."

"So I heard."

"How was your trip to New York?"

"It was nice. Got a chance to go to the Doug E. Fresh concert at Madison Square Garden. It was him, LL Cool J., and Eric B. & Rakim. Girl, that sexy ass LL Cool J. turned it out, fo' real! I brought you a present back."

"Did you?"

"You better believe it! You know I wasn't gonna forget about my girl. It's right outside, in the trunk of Ricky's car. So, Monica, what actually happened?"

"Nigga robbed me, Yolanda. I had to give up everything. Some tall, dark-skinned nigga. Did they tell you what the coward did to Ali?'

"No," said Yolanda. "What did he do?"

"The coward cut off Ali's left pinky finger and threatened to cut his throat if I didn't cooperate!"

Yolanda gasped in shock.

"Oh, my gosh. Where is my lil' man, anyway?"

"He's at my mother's place for the weekend. I swear, Yolanda, if I could've somehow gotten to my .38 revolver, which was in my glove compartment, I would've laid his ass out like the oriental rug on the floor in my living room. No jokin', yo!"

"I feel ya on that note, shit," said Yolanda, before turning her attention to Ricky as he walked into the room wit' a bacon, egg and cheese sandwich.

"You only fixed something for yourself?" asked Yolanda. "Is that how you doin' it now, Rick? Lookin' out fo' self."

"Look who's talking," replied Ricky. "You didn't bring me anything back from New York."

"Humph, for your information, I did bring you something back! I got gifts for you, Bootsy, and Monica. What you think in those bags of mine in the trunk of your car?"

Ricky looked over at Monica, who was searching for aspirin.

"Whatcha gon' do wit lil momma?"

Monica threw up her hands. "I ain't got nothing to do wit' that."

Yolanda walked over to Ricky and got in his face aggressively.

"Now give me a bite!"

"Here, Yolanda girl, looking like a chocolate foxy brown! You lucky we at Monica's crib. Or else I would rip you out of those tight ass jeans and make you say my name!"

Wit' what? Your tongue? 'Cause you ain't got no dick!"

"OUCH!" shouted Monica, adding fuel to the fire.

"Okay. We'll see later," said Ricky, before walking out.

Standing at the top of the stairway, Ricky called for Bootsy. He received no answer. So he headed back downstairs. He saw Bootsy knocked out on the sofa.

"Lil bruh tired as fuck," Ricky said to himself as he headed to his car to get the money he owed Monica.

****

"Girl, Yolanda, what's up wit you and Ricky? Y'all fuckin' now?' asked Monica.

"It ain't like that, believe me. You know how he is, though.

"Nah, I don't. Tell me."

"Like I said, it ain't like that. I let the nigga eat my pussy a couple of times and beat a little. He be wanting to get too seriously involved though, Monica. I ain't wit' all dat. Give niggas some pussy these days and they feel like they own ya! You know what I mean?"

"I hear ya."

Oh, but I know someone who has a serious THANG for you," said Yolanda.

"Who?"

"I can't tell ya right now."

They both heard Ricky stomping back up the steps. Monica lowered her voice.

"Come on now, Yolanda. You know you gotta tell me. Who is it?"

Before Yolanda could say anything else, Ricky entered the room. He handed Monica a brown paper bag. "You know what that is. It's a little under twenty-four grand. I still got a kilo of coke left. But I'll be finished wit' it probably no later than tomorrow or Monday."

"Alright," said Monica.

He looked in Yolanda's direction.

"You want me to drop you off at your place, or what? 'Cause I'm 'bout to bounce."

"Ricky, I'ma drop her off. I need her to help me wit' something while she's here," said Monica.

"Alright. C'mon then, Yolanda, and get your stuff out my car. Monica, I'll hit you on your pager later."

"Yeah, do that, bruh," she said as he and Yolanda made their way downstairs. Ricky tapped Bootsy on his leg.

"C' mon soldier, we 'bout to bounce."

****

Outside in Monica's driveway, Yolanda stood at the trunk of Ricky's

Cadillac. He opened it and she bent over to grab her belongings. As she did so, Ricky smacked her on her butt. "You betta not've been up there in New York giving my ass away to dem New York niggas," he said.

"Whatever! I know you better not hit me on my ass like that again. I'm dead serious, Ricky. Now here!" She pulled out a New York Knicks hooded jersey wit' a Starter cap to match.

"Don't ever say I ain't never done anything for ya, knucklehead!"

"I got your knucklehead," Ricky replied, while holding up his new 6X large hoody.

"Oh, but I ain't no New York Knicks' fan," he said.

Yolanda sucked her teeth. "Well, you are now."

Yolanda handed Bootsy his.

"You bought this for me?" Said Bootsy, checking out his hoody and cap. It was the same as Ricky's, only smaller.

"Of course. I couldn't forget my bruh."

"Yo, thanks, Yolanda. I appreciate you thinking of me."

"No problem, Bootsy. We family. But that nigga there," Yolanda pointed to Ricky, "ain't shit."

"You know I love you, girl. Come here," replied Ricky.

She looked at him and rolled her eyes. "Damn you," she said and headed back into Monica's crib.

"Dawg, y'all wild," Bootsy said to Ricky. "Wild as a muthafucka!"

CHAPTER EIGHT
(Annie Pearl's House)
The Talk

William had Emily drop him off at his Auntie Annie Pearl's house, where he had been since 8:00 a.m. Emily had to be at work by 9:00 a.m., at the Foot Locker in South Park Mall. After finishing some household chores, his Auntie Pearl called him into the kitchen. She was thawing out chicken that she intended to fry later.

"You hungry?" She asked."

"No, ma'am. Not really. Thirsty though."

She poured him a glass of homemade lemon tea as he took a seat at the table.

"Who was that white gal that dropped you off this morning?"

"A close friend of mine."

"How come you didn't bring her in to meet me?"

"It was still early and I didn't know whether or not you were still in bed."

"In the bed. Since when have you ever known me to sleep late? I still get up at the same time every morning—six o'clock."

"She had to get to work anyway, Auntie Pearl."

"So are the two of you dating?" she asked, before setting a tall, clear glass of lemon tea on the table before him and taking a seat directly across from him at the table.

"No, she's just someone nice that I met while I was in prison. We're just friends," he said.

"I started getting a little worried 'bout cha for a while there. You haven't been over to check on ya' old Auntie but twice since ya been out. Neither have you called. Now tell ya Auntie what's really going on wit'cha."

He took a drink of tea before commenting.

"I'm not gonna lie to you, Auntie Pearl. I've been here and there, doing what I do best. Hustling. I tried to get myself on the right track by getting a job and what not, but it wasn't easy. I mean, directly after I was released, I was informed that there was a construction site uptown that was hiring laborers. Since I am a certified welder, I thought maybe this was my opportunity to make me some money the right way. So I went and applied for a job, only to be told to return the following day. When I returned, the foreman there told me the guy who had requested that I come back was off for the next four days, and that they had stopped hiring. I asked him if there was anything he could do for me? He said that it simply was not his call. So I left and didn't bother returning again. I applied for other jobs, but got nuthin'. No one wants to hire a convicted felon. I didn't know nuthin' else to do, but start back hustling."

Annie Pearl reached across the table to grab his hand. She took a deep breath.

"Life is hard, son, everywhere you go. You and I have talked about this time and time again. If it ain't one thing, it's another. A trial here, a tribulation there, but something for sure. I've been on this earth sixty-seven years, sometimes having to bend my knees not just in prayer to God, but to scrub floors for white folks to make a few dollars. What had to be done, had to be done. Sometimes I would be scrubbing those floors for white folks and would hear some of them in passing on several occasions, referring to our people as niggers and other depreciative names. I never did let it cause me to feel belittled. I would just keep right on working, because sometimes, son, you gotta swallow your pride and see the bigger picture."

"Yeah, but times are different now. A young black man in this society wit' a felony on his record is doomed when it comes to scoring a decent job," said William.

"I'm aware of that, too. I watch the news every night. I see how the media stereotypes most young black males as being more violent and ignorant than they really are. And I don't like it. However, even in the face of this, you young people gotta believe in yourselves and, above all, y'all have got to become more patient. Patience is a virtue, son. Stop giving those white folks in high places a reason to put y'all in their jailhouses, and y'all stop treating one another so unkindly. I was at the market the other day and overheard these two young people conversing. They were calling one another niggers and what not. I wanted to grab the two of them and give them a good old fashioned butt whipping, because not only were they making themselves look bad, they were doing so without regard for who was in their presence. This is the type of nonsense that must stop," she concluded. She got up from the table to grab cooking oil from the cabinet for her chicken while William finished his tea.

"I agree with you, Auntie Pearl, even though I'm a part of the same negativity."

"Well, none of us are perfect. The Bible says all have sinned, so don't take it like I'm being judgmental. I'm not. I just wanna see you young people doing better."

"Oh, I know," he said, handing her his glass. She took it and held it up to her face. She didn't see a drop left in it, and smirked.

"Still love my lemon tea, huh?"

"Always will, Auntie Pearl. No one in the city makes it better. And, by the way, I brought you a lil' present."

"What is it?" she asked.

"Can't tell ya', but it's underneath your pillow," he replied. Then he got up, walked over to her and looked her squarely in the eyes.

"Auntie Pearl," he said, taking a deep breath, "all my life you've been there for me. You were there when no one else wanted to be, including my own biological mother and father, who abandoned me when I was an infant."

Tears began to well up in his eyes. One rolled down the bridge of his nose. "But you took me in. You did everything in your power to raise me right, and I appreciate it. Even when I got into trouble and was sent to prison, you visited me and sent me money. Even though I'm all grown up now, you have never once refused me a place to stay or food to eat. Thank you so much. And I want you to know that if I've ever hurt you in any way, or caused you to worry and stay up all times of the night, I apologize. Hurting you is the last thing I would ever want to do."

She took a handkerchief from her apron and wiped the tears that were flowing from his eyes. Then she placed the back of her hand to his forehead.

"You sure you okay today?" she asked jokingly, surprised to hear him express himself as he did.

"Everything's fine. I'm just happy right now. Happy to be here with you and happy that I can give you something to somewhat express my gratitude to you for loving me as you have over the years. I love you," he concluded, giving her a hug and kiss on the cheek.

******

William stepped outside onto his Auntie Annie Pearl's front porch to wait for his taxi. While there, he looked out over the neighborhood he'd grown up in and gotten his hustle on for many days and nights. He noticed how much things had changed. No more drug dealers, prostitutes and pimps hanging out, hustling on the corner of 5th and Trade Streets, the way they had been prior to him going off to state prison. No more paraphernalia, such as used drug needles, empty cocaine bags and crack pipes all over peoples' yards and driveways. Nothing but seemingly golden silence and a peaceful neighborhood for elders like his Auntie Annie Pearl to walk through safely. Also absent was the possibility of getting hit by some gunman's stray bullet.

All of the changes were the result of the CLEAN THE NEIGHBORHOOD OPERATION, headed by the Charlotte Police Department and the Housing Authority Officials. *My, my, my, how things have changed,* he thought.

******

"Someone called a taxi at ahhh, 229 Frazier Avenue?" shouted the taxi driver.

"Yeah," replied William, lifting his hands, before heading inside to grab some of his belongings.

"Auntie Annie Pearl, I'll see you later. Don't forget your present."

Later that evening, Annie Pearl checked under her pillow for her present. She discovered a white envelope wit' $10,000 enclosed and the words, *'With Love, Your Son,'* written on it.

Death, No Exceptions!

"The streets are icy cold, frosting with drugs, sex, and the violence of ruthless men. Yet the streets are not alone; this whole world is sin prone."

CHAPTER NINE
I Don't Forget No Faces!

"So you like the gift I bought you, Monica?" Yolanda asked, as they chilled at her apartment in Double Oaks.

"I love it," replied Monica. "Satin purple and white fish net panties and bra. Shit, what female of any class wouldn't? The only problem is who's gonna see me looking sexy in 'em? I haven't been with no one since the passing of Big Jay-Jay."

"You got niggas in the Queen City dying to see you in something like that. I know one in particular," said Yolanda.

"There you go again, stirring my curiosity. Are you gonna tell me who this mystery person is, or not?"

"It's a person you would least expect to have a thing for you."

"WHO IS IT, YOLANDA?"

"It's Bootsy."

"Bootsy! Yeah right," said Monica, putting her hands on her hips. "What would he know to do wit' all of this?"

"I don't know what he would do wit' it. I just know if he was given the opportunity he probably would end up becoming a person you would easily fall in love wit'."

"'Cause, believe it or not, Monica, he's not only cute, he's respectful and focused."

"Maybe so, but he's never given me any indication that he likes me," said Monica.

"Yeah, probably because he doesn't want Ricky to know. They're tight and you know Ricky loves the hell out of you. Bootsy is smart. He knows steppin' to you wit' how he feels may ruin his and Ricky's brotherhood. So he keeps quiet about it. He only told me, because he and I kick it like that."

"Doesn't he have a girl, though?"

"Humph," replied Yolanda, sucking her teeth. "I doubt it! Hell, all he really does is hustle twenty-four-seven wit' Ricky. And you know yourself that he's a lil' gangsta! Shit, what young chick his age is ready for him?"

"I hear ya."

"Keep all that between you and me though, Monica. I know how you are. You'll let the rabbit out the hat in a minute!"

Monica stared at Yolanda.

"Look who's talking. I've heard enough. Girl, get in there and take your bath, so we can roll on up out of here."

****

As Yolanda prepared to bathe, Monica went into Yolanda's bedroom to check herself out in the huge mirror over the dresser.

She picked through her braids with her fingers, while looking at her reflection in the mirror. *Damn, I gotta get my darn braids done over,* she realized, seeing that her weaved-in extensions were old looking from being in nearly two weeks already. She continued tightening up her sexy look by putting on a little black eyeliner and lipstick. Then she scanned the many pictures Yolanda had in the room, most of which were flicks of her and Yolanda when they were in high school or at the club. One picture in particular caught her eye. It was one of Yolanda next to a guy who resembled the guy who robbed her. She grabbed it from the dresser for closer inspection, before storming into the bathroom with it in her hand.

"Yolanda, this nigga looks identical to the one who robbed me!"

"Who?" shouted Yolanda, with bubble bath all over her.

Monica held up the picture in Yolanda's face.

"William?" Yolanda said. "Hell naw, he couldn't hurt a flea!"

"Well, the bastard hurt my son and stuck me up! I don't forget no faces. Now where the fuck you know him from?"

Yolanda cut her bath short, hopped out of the tub, and began drying off.

"I met him at the Jaguar Club back in the day. The nigga just got out the joint. He ain't been on the streets in almost four years. But somehow he got my address and popped up over here one evening. He didn't have nothing, so I broke him off a few hundred dollars. We may have seen each other two or three more times after that. That was probably three weeks ago. I haven't heard anything from him since. Are you sure it's him, Monica? 'Cause I'm telling you, this dude is soft as cotton."

Monica looked at the picture again as they headed back into Yolanda's bedroom.

"Yo, it's him, Yolanda. I'm confident."

"We gon' find out. I got his pager number over there in my phonebook," said Yolanda while dressing.

Monica walked over to the telephone.

"Who you 'bout to call?"

"Ricky," said Monica angrily.

"No, Monica. Don't call Ricky. Fuck that! Don't call nobody. If this is in fact the nigga who robbed you, then we gon' handle it. You and I!"

"You and I? Whatcha' mean, you and I?"

"Just what I said. Look, we got to stop always depending on the guys to handle for us what we are capable of handling ourselves. Now either we're solid or soft. I'm solid," said Yolanda.

"Shit, I'm solid!" replied Monica.

"Alright then," said Yolanda, giving Monica some dap. "Hand me that phonebook over there. Let me see if I can't contact this nigga!"

CHAPTER TEN 10
Do Me Like You Did My Cousin!

Back at Emily's crib, William stepped in on Rachael rollin' a blunt in the kitchen.

"Looks like I came back at the right time, huh?"

She looked over her shoulder at him. "Gosh, you scared me. How long have you been standing there?"

"Long enough to see that you're gonna need help smoking that blunt. Can I fire it up?"

She handed it to him. "Why not," she said, seeing him digging deep into his pocket for his lighter. He found it and lit the blunt, taking only a puff to ensure that it was lit without purposely inhaling. He handed it back to her.

"Ladies first," he said. She smirked, and then took a pull of the blunt, as William looked on waiting for her to choke from its potency. She hit it again before passing it to him.

"Damn, Miss Savannah Georgia, how long have you been smoking this shit?"

She laughed. "Ever since I was ten.My father grows it."

He took a few pulls. "It's some good ass shit. I know that much. Here."

He attempted to hand it back, but she waved her hand, indicating she'd had enough. "That's not the kind of grass you can smoke all up. A puff or two will leave you fucked up, trust me," said Rachael.

"Hell, I believe ya. I can feel that shit already. You wanna do me a favor?"

"What?"

"You wanna help me bag up something?"

"Something like what?"

William nodded his head. "Come to Emily's room. Let me show you."

William went straight to the closet and grabbed the pillowcase. He took out one of the Ziploc bags of coke. Rachael's eyes got big. "This is what I was talking about. Can you help me bag some of this up?"

Rachael hesitantly shook her head. "I can't touch that stuff," she said. "Because if Emily comes in and catches me, I'm dead!"

"Well, you ain't gotta worry about her catching you, 'cause, for one, she don't get off work 'til five o'clock.

It's only twenty after four. Two people bagging this shit up will only take fifteen minutes, tops."

She thought about it for a second.

"What is it I would actually have to do?" she asked, sitting on Emily's bed with her elbows on her knees and her chin in her palm.

"All I want you to do is tie the bags."

"Okay. Hand me the bags," she said.

"I gotta go into the kitchen and get them. Hold tight. I'll be right back."

******

When William returned from the kitchen, he found Rachael lying back, looking up at the ceiling. Her legs were gapped open wide enough for him to notice that she had slipped her panties off. "What the fuck?" he said to himself.

"Do me like you did my cousin," she said, still looking up at the ceiling.

William was speechless.

"I said I want you to do me like you did my cousin."

"Rachael, who are you talking to?" he asked, feeling his nature rising at the same time.

Rachael lifted her shirt to expose her titties.

"I saw what you did to my cousin. Now do the same to me," she said, caressing her titties.

"What did you see me do to your cousin, Rachael?" asked William.

"I saw how you were throwing that dick of yours in her, making her feel good. I wanna feel good, too," she said. Then she sat up and reached for his penis, unzipping his jeans to get to it. Once she did, she wasted no time putting it in her mouth. It felt so good to him, he forgot all about bagging cocaine.

******

Right about the time William was nearing ejaculation, Rachael eased up.

"You like that, Daddy?" she asked, looking up at him.

"I love it, Ma. Do your thang," William said.

With his penis still in her hand, she lay back on the bed in the missionary position and placed the head of his penis to her kitty lips. She rolled it around her clitoris. Then she placed her legs in the buck for him to completely have his way. He thrust his penis in her, but quickly pulled it out after hearing keys jingling.

"Oh, shit," he said. "Rachael, go to the bathroom and lock the door behind you."

William headed toward the living room, straightening his jeans along the way.

It was Emily. William met her just as she walked through the door.

"What's up, boo?" he asked.

"Tired as the fuck. Here, grab these bags. Why the hell are you sweating like that?" asked Emily.

"'Cause I had to rush over here to start bagging coke. Plus, your air conditioner's off," he replied.

"Smells like weed in here. Who been smoking?"

"Rachael and I lit one. Well, she was actually rolling a blunt when I arrived, and she let me take a drag or two."

"Fuckin' no wonder your eyes so red. Where's Rachael anyway?"

"Probably back there in the bathroom. I don't know. Like I said, I was in the process of bagging coke."

"Well, try those sneakers on to see if they fit. You did say 11½, right?"

"Right," replied William.

"I got you the new Air Jordans and two pairs of Air Force Ones, with sweat suits to match."

William tried a sneaker on.

"The Jordans fit perfectly, boo. Thanks."

"The other one should, too. By the way, I hollered at a friend of mine named JD earlier. He's interested in copping a whole kilo. I told him that as soon as I spoke with you, I would give him a call. That's why I got off early."

"You told him who I was?"

"Do I look that stupid? C'mon now, never would I reveal who my people are," replied Emily.

"Well, give the cat a call. Let him know you got it and it's going for twenty-seven grand. Twenty for me and seven for you."

Emily made the call and JD instructed her to meet him at one of his spots off of South Boulevard, behind the Queens Park Movie Theater.

******

Emily headed to her bedroom, but stopped at the bathroom first to pee. The door was closed. She knocked, but got no answer.

"Rachael? Rachael, are you in there?"

Still no answer. Emily turned the doorknob. Seeing it was unlocked, she entered. "Damn, girl, what the fuck are you doing?" shouted Emily, witnessing Rachael laid out in the bathtub. She stepped toward her and shook her arm.

"Rachael, get up!"

William heard Emily shouting and walked in. "What's wrong wit' her?"

"She's fucked up from that blunt y'all smoked. Every time she smokes that shit she does this," said Emily.

William gave her a hand getting Rachael up. "C'mon, Rachael, girl. We about to take a ride."

"A ride where?" asked Rachael, in a slurred voice.

"A ride around town. You need some fresh air, anyway," Emily replied.

******

As Emily and Rachael headed out, William got a page. The number looked familiar, but he couldn't recall whose it was. He grabbed Emily's home phone and dialed the number.

"Hello?" answered a female after the first ring.

"Yes, ah, did someone from this number page William?"

"Hell, what, you don't know my number when you see it?"

"Who is this?"

"This Yolanda, boy, quit playin'."

"Oh, shit, girl, what's up?"

"You know me, chillin'. Just got in from New York?"

"When, just now?"

"Yeah, been gone two weeks," she said, lying.

"You talked to anybody since you been back?"

"Nope. I told myself that I wasn't gonna let anybody know that I was back 'til after the weekend was over."

"What made you call me?" asked William.

"I was looking at the picture that you and I took when I visited you at Camp Green. Looking at it made me think about you."

"Is that right?"

"Urnmm, hummm."

"You know I got a settlement, right?"

"A settlement? What kind of settlement?" asked Yolanda.

"It's from a lawsuit I had pending, from when I was in prison. Some guards jumped on me and some other prisoners. They finally settled," he lied.

"You never told me anything about that."

"It happened when I was in Central Prison. The judge awarded me $50,000."

"Wow," said Yolanda. "Break ya girl off something then."

"You name it, you can get it. Shit, you looked out for me when I got out of prison. A nigga owe you," he said.

"Nah, you don't owe me nothing."

'Yeah, da fuck I do, too. Hell, you helped me out, Yolanda."

"Nah, you alright. Your girl could use a fat blunt though, right about now," said Yolanda.

"Shit, if that's all you want, I got plenty. I ain't talking about no bullshit, either. I got some grass that'll make you wanna do the nasty!"

Yolanda laughed, while Monica looked on.

"Yeah, right, boy," she said. "Then bring your girl some and let's see."

"I might slide through."

"What you mean you might slide through? Hell, ain't nothing to it, but to do it, unless you got some other chick you gotta be wit'."

"Like I said, Yolanda, I might slide through."

"So what you saying? You don't wanna see your girl?"

Ever since Yolanda was a teenager she'd known just how to manipulate guys that she felt were suckers.

"Baby, you know I wanna see you and break you off somethin'"

Yolanda cut him off before he could finish his sentence.

"Yo, you gon' come or not? Shit, I ain't trying to be waiting up all night on a train that ain't comin'."

"I'll be there. Just be looking for me," he concluded. He was totally naïve about her true intentions.

CHAPTER ELEVEN
You Got Game

"Damn, lil' momma," Monica said to Yolanda, "you got game like a muthafucka, mo' game than the Charlotte Hornets."

"Nah, it's like I told you, the nigga green as spring grass. A fuckin' wanna-be ass gangsta."

"Alright now, Yolanda," said Monica, "you know a wanna-be is a gonna-be. Shit, the nigga had to have some type of guts. He took what I had and cut my damn son's finger off."

"The muthafucka was hungry and desperate. You put the two together and you'll get someone who'll do something stupid like he did. And guess what he had the fuckin' nerve to tell me?"

"What?" asked Monica, fully-attentive.

"He had the nerve to tell me that he was just awarded a $50,000 settlement from a lawsuit."

"Awarded $50,000 from a lawsuit?" shouted Monica, repeating Yolanda.

"Yeah. The nigga is so stupid he thinks everyone else is as stupid as he is. He says it's from a lawsuit filed while he was in prison, from a prison guard beating his ass."

"Humph, I can't believe he told you that shit," said Monica with her arms crossed.

"Yep, but you know what? That's confirmation that he is the one, which is also why you're going to have to do something about yo' Benz outside. If the stupid ass nigga does come over here and spot it, he's gonna know something's up."

"Yeah, you right. But shit, don't sweat that, just follow me back to my crib in your car and we'll shoot right back over here in yours, you feel me?" said Monica.

"Sounds good to me," replied Yolanda.

Monica walked over to Yolanda's living room sofa, grabbed her money green Gucci bag and pulled out her .38 revolver. She opened the chamber to check for bullets. It was fully loaded. Then she put the snubbed-nose barrel to her lips and kissed it.

"I just wanna be able to look that muthafucka in his face and ask him one question," said Monica.

"And what would that be, Monica?"

"You'll see. C'mon, let's go!"

CHAPTER TWELVE
Snaggle Cat

Ricky and Bootsy were across town, on the south side of Charlotte in the Brent Hill apartment complex off of Remount Road. They were doing what they did best, clocking dollars. They were hustling out of a chick's house, whom they called "Snaggle Cat." Snaggle Cat, whose real name was Patricia Page, was a forty-three-year-old crack addict. She'd been smoking on the so-called glass dick since 1988 when she first learned of cooking powder cocaine with baking soda.

Unlike most crack addicts, who were unusually slim, frail and just bummed-out looking, like they'd been smoking for days on end and getting high without any sleep, Snaggle Cat was unbelievably thick. She weighed nearly 230 pounds and stood about about five-foot-six. She resembled Nell Carter from the television sitcom, *Gimme a Break!* The only visible difference was that Snaggle Cat's two front teeth were missing, hence, her nickname. She didn't seem to give a damn, though. Ricky had offered several times to pay for her to see a dentist, who could hook her up with a nice partial, but she always refused.

She and Ricky were in the kitchen and Snaggle Cat had just finished cooking up half a kilo, which was her primary job. She decided to smoke a piece. While Ricky looked on, she put a fat piece in her pipe and hit it, using her lighter to melt the coke into the stem. Then she inhaled deeply and held it for about five seconds before lifting her head to release the smoke from her lungs. Ricky shook his head.

"Damn, Snaggle Cat, when are you gonna cut this shit loose? Hell, you could make a killin' if you do."

"When...you...stop...sellin' it," she replied, finding it hard to get her words out. She was feeling the spontaneous effects of the cocaine rush, which was also causing her mouth to twist sideways.

"I wanna get off of this shit badder than you may think, Ricky. But you know what? This shit is a monster. It'll rob you of your strength, will, and better judgment, and will have you doing things you never ever thought of doing. No bullshit. One time, probably about a year before I met you, I had my little nieces over here with me and I was feening for a hit so bad that I allowed a guy whom I didn't even really know to have sex with me. I was wearing a sundress at the time. Honestly, I'll never forget it. The guy pulled my sundress up, right in the presence of my nieces and started having sex with me. He was so rough that my little nieces started crying, assuming that I was under attack. And—"

Ricky waved his hands and shook his head. "That's enough, Snaggle Cat. I can't stand to hear stuff like that. Some of these sorry muthafuckas out here are worse than the crack we sell," he said. Immediately after conveying that thought to her, his pager went off. It was Monica. He phoned her without delay, using Snaggle Cat's kitchen phone.

"What's up, Monica?"

"Nothing much, bruh. Just checking up on you and Bootsy. What y'all doin'?"

"You know we holding things down, getting money, baby girl. You and Yolanda still together?"

"Yeah. I'm in her car right now. We on our way to her crib. You wanna holler at her?"

"Hell, yeah, put her crazy ass on the phone."

Monica covered her cell phone with her hand. "Ricky wanna holler at cha, Yolanda. You wanna holler at him?" Yolanda shook her head no.

"She ain't trying to holler right now, Ricky. What's up with y'all two, anyway?"

"Yolanda's trippin'. That's what's up," said Ricky.

"Oh, is that what she's doin'?"

"Yeah, but peep this, I still haven't heard anything on that robbery thang. We over here keeping our ears open, though."

"Right, right," replied Monica, following Yolanda's advice by keeping to herself what she had already discovered about the thug who robbed her. "Something will come up. Yeah, something will come up real soon."

"You sound confident."

"Well, it's just what I believe and hope, Ricky. That's all. Where's Bootsy?"

"He's outside. What's up? You want to speak with him?"

"I'll speak with him later, but do tell him I'm sorry for yelling at him last night. I was just a little frustrated, that's all."

"Bet," said Ricky.

"Y'all call me in a few hours. I'll be at Yolanda's place more than likely, a'ight?"

"A'ight, sis. I love you, girl."

"What? You gettin' sentimental on me now, Ricky?"

"Nah, you my sister, and I just wanted you to know that. Something wrong with that?"

"No, boo. I'm just messing with you. I love you, too."

******

After hanging up the telephone, Ricky headed outside to holler at Bootsy. Besides things going well as far as them making money was concerned, Ricky was still overwhelmingly frustrated at not hearing anything about the robbery from any of his associates around the city. He pondered on the matter for a moment, then found himself temporarily thinking of little Ali and how he must've been feeling as a result of the encounter. Not to mention, for the rest of Ali's life, he'd bear a scar that would remind him of the horrible event.

"Ricky, what's on your mind?" asked Snaggle Cat, totally snapping him out of the thoughts racing through his head.

"Ain't nothing," he lied.

"Then why are you standing by the door all dazed out lookin'? You look like you don' had you a hit of this crack," said Snaggle Cat jokingly.

"Yeah, right, I'm straight," he replied, before heading out the door in Bootsy's direction.

******

"What it look like out here, dawg?" asked Ricky.

"Look like money, my nigga. These fiends out here running like Carl Lewis for this crack. What's up with you? You look tired," said Bootsy.

"Shit, I just got off the phone with Monica."

"Okay, how she holding up?"

"She sounds good. Her and Yolanda still hanging out. She told me to tell you that she was sorry for yelling at you last night."

Bootsy smirked. "She told you to tell me that, huh?"

"Yep."

"Ricky, bruh, you know what? I like Monica a whole lot. Man, that sista smart, but what I like most is her ability to keep her business to herself. Some girls talk too damn much. Not Monica, though. I think that's important. But check this out. I was thinking about what Monica told us while we were at her crib last night."

"What's that?" asked Ricky.

"Remember when she said that she didn't know how that nigga who robbed her managed to creep up on her like he did?"

"Yeah, I remember," replied Ricky with his ear attentive to what Bootsy had to say.

"Hell, I was wondering about the same shit. I thought about it over and over again late last night and today. Think about it, bruh. Monica don't hang out or associate with virtually nobody but us—you, me, and Yolanda. Other niggas in this city don't know she got coke and money. Only you, me, and Yolanda know that shit. So whoever robbed Monica, in my opinion, had to get their information about her from one of us. We already know both of us can be eliminated, 'cause we pretty much know how these niggas are out here."

"So, what are you implying, bruh?"

"What I'm implying is, Yolanda, dawg. As much as I love her and will kill any nigga out here in these streets who would violate her, she tend to run her mouth too much."

"You feel Yolanda may have had something to do with Monica getting robbed?"

Death, No Exceptions!

"All I'm saying is loose lips sink ships, and that's real talk, Ricky. In my opinion, we all need to meet and see what's really behind this robbery shit," concluded Bootsy.

"You got a helluva point. I'll call Monica later and relay that recommendation," said Ricky.

"Do dat, my nigga. Yeah, do dat."

CHAPTER THIRTEEN
Emily

"Yo, William, my friend, JD, couldn't believe how raw that coke was," said Emily, handing William twenty-seven grand. He gave her seven grand for making the transaction.

"He liked that shit, huh?" asked William.

"Yo, he even said that he's gonna want to buy more in a couple days."

"Good. That's more money for us, right?"

"Believe that. Guess what he did, though?"

"What he did, baby?"

"He had one of the crack heads who work for him to cook the coke up and test it right in front of me. In a matter of minutes, William, I lie to you not, the crack head's eyes got big. He started peeping out of the windows and shit. Then the muthafucka started comin' out of his clothes. I asked JD what the hell was going on and he told me that's what that crack head does when he has smoked some good cocaine."

William laughed.

"I had never seen anyone act like that. Honestly, it scared the fuck out of me," said Emily.

"Where was Rachael?"

"I left her in my jeep. Yo, she was knocked the fuck out anyway. Didn't have a clue as to where she was at. Look at her."

Emily pointed to Rachael on the couch.

"Looks like she's had too much to smoke. She'll be a'ight, just let her sleep it off. I know one thing, Emily, I need a book bag. Do you have an extra one?"

"I should have another one hanging up in my closet. Let me see."

She walked into her bedroom with William following close behind. His plan was to stash all of his money in the book bag and carry it with him. He had already phoned for a taxi, which would be arriving any minute.

"Emily, I gotta handle some business across town. Somebody paged me right before you came in. I probably won't be back 'til tomorrow sometime, so I'm leaving the coke here. When I do get back, I want to talk to you about this candy apple red Nissan 300ZX I saw on a lot for sale. I'ma need you to purchase it for me in your name."

"That won't be a problem. Did you check for the price?" asked Emily.

"Yeah, it was on the window. They want $6,500 for it."

"Sounds like your taxi out there. I hear a horn blowing. Hold on..." said Emily, as she walked into the living room to look out of the window. After a few seconds, William headed in the direction of the living room, carrying the book bag on his shoulder. "It is your taxi, baby," said Emily. "Be careful, alright?"

"I will," replied William, giving her a kiss on the lips.

"You sure you don't want me to come with you?"

"Nah, I'ma be at a gambling house," he lied. "You don't wanna be hanging around a spot like that all night."

"Okay. Then just call if you need me for anything."

****

(12:23 a.m.   Back at Yolanda's Place)

"So where you think I should be hiding when he comes over here, Yolanda?" asked Monica.

Yolanda got up from sitting on her bed and looked around. "I think you should hide in the closet. What you think?"

"Shit. For real, for real, I was actually thinking about the bathroom."

"The bathroom? Why the bathroom?"

"That way I can maybe catch him with his dick in his hands."

"Girl, cut the jokes," said Yolanda.

"Do it look like I'm jokin'? I'm as serious as a heart attack."

Yolanda paid the statement little attention. She had other things on her mind that she wanted to share with Monica. She walked over to her dresser and opened one of the drawers. She pulled out a burner that not even Monica was aware she had. "Do you know what this is, Monica?" Yolanda held it up for a better view.

Monica looked over at it and smacked her lips. "Of course I know what it is. It's a gun."

"Yeah, but do you know what kind of gun?"

"Looks like one of those .380 automatics."

"Damn, girl, you know your guns, huh?"

"Well, I recognize that kind, 'cause I used to have one. Big Jay-Jay gave it to me. It was chrome with a pearl handle just like that one. But he took it back and gave me the .38 revolver. He said he didn't want me carrying an automatic weapon, because they tend to jam up and shit."

"I ain't never had that problem out of this one," said Yolanda.

"Shoot it enough times and you will."

"You know why I bought it though, Monica?"

"I assume for your protection."

"Damn right. Cause a girl out here hustling ain't got no business doing so without one." Yolanda cocked the gun, thereby putting a bullet in the chamber. Monica looked on. "These steel things will bring a girl respect out here, no bullshit!"

"I ain't looking for any respect," said Monica. "I'm looking for revenge."

"Revenge?"

"Yeah, that's all I'm after—revenge," said Monica, before both of them heard the doorbell ring.

******

"Monica, get in the closet," said Yolanda with her voice low.

Yolanda put her .380 automatic back into the dresser drawer and headed toward the door to answer it. She knew it was William from looking through the peephole, so she tried calming herself enough to welcome him inside.

"Whatz up, stranger?" said Yolanda, giving William a big hug as he made his way into her living room.

"I'm a'ight. Thought I wasn't coming over, didn't you? I know you did," he said, smiling from ear to ear.

"Well, it ain't like you been over here lately. Honestly, I didn't know what to expect. You're looking good, though. But what's wit' the book bag?"

William took a seat and put the book bag between his legs. "Just some of my belongings. I thought I'd crash over here, if you don't mind."

"You know I don't mind. Go on and make yourself at home. You want something to drink?"

"Yeah. Hell, why not?"

Yolanda went into the kitchen, opened her frig and grabbed two big bottles of Boone's Farm, one for him and the other for her. When she returned, she saw about two ounces of weed on her living room table. She placed the bottle on the table next to the weed for him. "Damn, boy," she said with excitement, as she stared at the weed. "I thought you were bullshittin' about having plenty of that shit."

"I ain't playin' wit' cha. We gonna have us some fun tonight. I'm warning you though, this some high powered shit."

"Oh, really?" Yolanda opened her bottle of Boone's Farm. She started gulping it down like water, nearly drinking half of it her first turn up.

William opened his.

"I love Strawberry Boone's Farm," he said after taking a drink.

"It's my favorite, too."

"So why you standing up, Yolanda? Have a seat next to me, baby, and fire this up."

William passed her a joint.

"This ain't no blunt," she said.

"Exactly. Trust me, you can't handle a blunt of this shit."

"Well, if you say so."

She lit it up, but didn't take a big drag, because she wanted to remain as clearheaded as possible, for whatever may happen.

She then passed it to him. He took a couple of big drags and passed it back.

Again she took only a small pull.

"Do me a favor, Yolanda?"

"What," she replied, before handing him what remained of the joint.

"Take your blouse off."

Yolanda looked at him, distraught. "Take my blouse off? Damn boy, you just got here thirty minutes ago and you want me to take my blouse off?"

"I don't mean any harm by it, baby. I just thought that since only the two of us are here, you wouldn't mind loosening up a little," he said while removing his Air Nike dark gray, white and black hoody and the T-shirt underneath it. Yolanda shook her head and finished off her Boone's Farm. Then she removed her blouse to fulfill his wishes. To his surprise, she was braless and as his nature would have it, he caught a hard-on.

CHAPTER FOURTEEN
In The Closet

In the closet of Yolanda's bedroom, Monica waited anxiously. All she could seem to picture in her mind while doing so was the moment her son Ali was screaming in pain from William cutting off his pinky finger. The thought so painfully intense, it not only made her grip her .38 revolver, but it also made her want to burst out of the closet and just bumrush him.

Seconds after contemplating those thoughts, she felt her pager vibrating. She checked to see who it was. By the code '222' she knew it was Ricky. He also put the code '911' behind his code to let Monica know it was an emergency. "Ricky picked a fine time to page me," she said to herself. She checked her watch. It was 1:19am. Due to the situation, she was unable to answer him back directly. Plus, she had left her cell phone on Yolanda's dresser. Her pager continued to vibrate. She felt it wouldn't be long before her cell phone started ringing. About three full minutes elapsed before what she suspected was confirmed. She heard her phone ring about four times before hearing Yolanda approach to answer it.

******

Curious as to what was being discussed over the phone, Monica placed her ear to the closet door. That did her no good, because Yolanda was not talking as loudly as she normally did. The conversation lasted a minute or two. Then, to Monica's surprise, she heard the voice of the guy whom she had become all too familiar with. "Yolanda, where's your bathroom at? This Boone's Farm got my bladder full as hell," William shouted.

Monica's heart nearly skipped a beat and her knees began to quiver. She pulled her .38 revolver out and pressed it against her leg.

"The bathroom is down the hall to your left," shouted Yolanda in response to William. Monica kept her ear to the door for any chance of him coming closer. But William headed straight to the bathroom, while Yolanda snuck and paid her a visit in the closet. "Look, Ricky just called. He asked to speak with you, claiming that it was an emergency. I told him we were in the middle of something and that we would call him back in about an hour."

"What's up with that nigga in there?" asked Monica.

"He ain't got a clue what's going on. I want you to come out and surprise his ass when you hear my stereo come on."

Monica nodded her head. "What the hell is your blouse doin' off?"

"That ain't important right now. Just do what I told you," said Yolanda, checking to see if William was coming.

"Well, hurry up," said Monica. "'Cause, shit, I gotta pee."

******

Before Yolanda could close the closet door and head back into her living room, William came out of the bathroom and went into Yolanda's bedroom.

He threw himself back onto her queen-sized bed like a kid without a worry in the world, with his body stretched out and arms spread. He lay there, staring at the ceiling as if in a trance. William was definitely feeling the effects of the marijuana.

So was Yolanda, who moved toward him at a snail's pace, trying to look sexy. Through a crack in the closet door, Monica could clearly spot the two of them. She saw William with one of Yolanda's nipples in his mouth. And Yolanda looked to be enjoying it.

Feeling her patience wearing thin, Monica cocked the hammer back on her .38 revolver. "It's either now or never," she said to herself before easing the closet door open enough to step forward. Yolanda noticed her immediately and stepped aside. Monica caught William's attention when she pointed the barrel of her gun directly at his temple.

Shock, fear and trepidation gripped him, and he found himself wetting his pants uncontrollably.

"Get yo' punk ass off that bed and on yo' knees, muthafucka," commanded Monica.

The look on her face was different from the soft, sweet, ladylike look he had beheld and had under his control a few days ago. He knew she was serious. Therefore, he took no chances. "Yolanda, you set me up," he said distraughtly, making his way to his knees.

"Shut the fuck up and look at me, muthafucka!" shouted Monica.

William lifted his head. He felt so ashamed and disgraced for allowing himself to be played into this situation by Yolanda, that lifting his head took more courage than robbing Monica had.

"You fuckin' cut my son's finger off, punk, and now you gotta answer for that shit.

Do you know what that means, muthafucka? Huh?" Monica bit down on her bottom lip.

"I didn't mean to, Monica. I swear I didn't. Please don't shoot me," he pleaded, fearing for his life. Monica wanted to put one in his head, but before making that a reality, she had one question to ask him. The question had been on her mind from day one.

"How in the fuck did you know of me and my whereabouts?"

William looked over at Yolanda who was standing next to Monica with her blouse still off. She was as high as the sky. As much as he hated snitching, something he had not done since embracing the street way of life years ago, it was his firm belief that a friend should never rat on a friend. William had truly considered Yolanda his friend. But under the deception of such consideration, he now found himself in the shadow of death. For the first time in his life he broke a code that he had long embraced without compromise.

"Your friend told me everything. Didn't you, Yolanda?" said William.

"Nigga, you lying like the devil," she said, before making her way toward her dresser drawer to retrieve her .380 automatic. Monica stopped her before she got the chance, by firing a shot in the floor near her feet.

"Get yo' ass back over here before I fry yo' ass, and I ain't playin'," shouted Monica.

Yolanda stood still with her hands on her hips. "You gon' believe this nigga over me?"

"Bitch, I said get yo' ass over here. Matter of fact, get on yo' knees, too."

As Yolanda proceeded to follow Monica's orders, William jumped up from the floor and reached for the gun in Monica's hand. Without hesitation, Monica fired a single shot. The bullet grazed William on the side of his neck. He went down as fast as he had gotten up. He lay on the floor, gurgling as though drowning in his own blood. There was no doubt in Monica's mind that he was dying. She refocused her attention on Yolanda with seriousness of heart. "You better get to talking bitch, 'cause I'm a bullet away from giving you the same thing."

"Monica, please, we've been friends too long. Don't let your emotions override your intellect."

"Don't let my emotions override my intellect? You got some fuckin' nerve, bitch. You should've thought about that shit when your mouth was running my business to this nigga here, like it had diarrhea."

"Damn, Monica, it was an honest mistake. Shit, we all make 'em. I'm sorry, a'ight. I assure you it won't happen again," Yolanda pleaded.

"Fuck that! What you did was more than a damn honest mistake. It was a fatal one." Monica had more rage in her heart than she could cage. "Now my damn son gotta go through life missing a finger."

Tears began flowing from Monica's eyes. They ran freely down her face like never before, causing her to barely see Yolanda's face.

"You are no good to me," Monica said as she positioned her gun to Yolanda's head. At that point, Yolanda started crying. She couldn't believe what was happening. She and Monica had grown up together and were the best of friends. But by the killer look in Monica's eyes, a look that Yolanda had never seen her display, she knew Monica now saw her as an enemy. So Yolanda pleaded for her life all the more.

"Please, Monica," pleaded Yolanda. "Please don't do—"

Bam! Monica pulled the trigger before her friend could finish her sentence. She shot Yolanda in the middle of her forehead. Yolanda's body went totally limp as death overtook her.

Then Monica set Yolanda's apartment on fire and exited into the darkness of the early morning. She had no earthly idea of the thousands of dollars William had brought along in his book bag. Thousands that really belonged to her, but were now burning to ashes. Nor did Monica care. Her only concern was REVENGE, not riches. Revenge burned in her heart like a mighty burning furnace ignited by gasoline, which could only be quenched by squeezing the trigger on both William and Yolanda without compromise. And although what she did would forever leave her hands stained with blood that nothing could ever cleanse her hands of, she wasted no time pondering such reality. Instead, Monica hurried to the nearest payphone to call Ricky.

****

Ricky was at Snaggle Cat's place, drinking and gambling, when he got Monica's phone call. "Hello?" he answered after the first ring.

"Ricky, look, bro, I'm in the parking lot of Fatman's Beef & Fish Market off Stateville Drive. I need you to come get me immediately. I'm out here by myself," said Monica.

"By yourself?! What in the—?" Monica cut Ricky off. "Look, bro, don't ask me any questions. Just come get me," Monica suggested.

"At least tell me what's up," requested Ricky. "Are you alright, or what?"

"Hell, fuckin' no, I'm not alright!" Monica shouted, before violently slamming the phone down. She bowed her head, leaned against the phone booth, and started weeping hard. The murder of her best friend was beginning to sink into every fiber of her being. And it was far more than she imagined she could bear.

******

THE AFTERMATH
"When it rains, it pours."

CHAPTER FIFTEEN
Where's Yolanda?

Nearly twenty minutes after Monica phoned Ricky, he and Bootsy arrived at her location. Bootsy quickly jumped out of the car and told Monica to get into the front seat while he hopped into the back.

As Ricky drove off, they could all clearly hear the sirens from the fire department vehicles rushing past them. But among them, only Monica knew for certain the direction in which those vehicles were heading. Before she was comfortably seated, Ricky spoke his mind. "What in the hell you doing out here by yourself, Monica? And where's Yolanda?"

"She's dead," replied Monica, teary-eyed and running her hands over her braids nervously. "She's dead."

"Dead!" shouted Ricky in disbelief. "Yeah, right, Monica. Be for real now. Where is she? 'Cause I honestly don't like the idea of you being out here alone."

Monica lifted her hand as if she was about to be sworn in under oath for a very important office. "I kid you not. She's dead. Her and the punk ass muthafucka who robbed me! How about, Yolanda knew of this dude the whole damn time. She the one who hipped him to me. The punk told me while pleading for his life, right before I shot his ass. Look at this shit."

Monica pulled the picture of Yolanda and William together from the front pocket of her jeans. Monica had held onto it from the day she first beheld it. There was no way she was ever gonna let go of it, until she finally got the chance to confront her robber face-to-face.

Monica passed the picture to Ricky. He took it, but his eyes were too blurred from drinking over at Snaggle Cat's place to get a good visual.

85

Ricky honestly didn't want to view the picture anyway. The last thing he wanted to behold, drunk or sober, was his sweetheart, Yolanda, next to another man. So he faked a peep at it, and then handed it to Bootsy, who was more than eager to view it. Bootsy leaned toward the window in hopes of catching more light for a clearer view. As he focused in on the picture, he could see Yolanda hugged up next to Monica's robber. Beholding this dude made Bootsy grit his teeth in anger, because Bootsy wanted to be the one to burst William's bubble for the violation he had committed.

Damn, Bootsy thought to himself, *Damn! Damn! Damn!*

He shifted his attention to Yolanda in the picture. Considering that she was now allegedly deceased, his heart became secretly sorrowful. But rather than sob, he leaned forward and returned the picture to Monica. Bootsy placed his hand on her shoulder as a show of his support.

"It is what it is," said Bootsy. "I only have one disregard in the matter, Monica."

"What's that?" asked Monica, turning toward his direction.

"I only hate that you didn't call me to do your dirty work."

Ricky caught on to the comment expeditiously. Hate that Monica didn't call him to do her dirty work. What the fuck did Bootsy mean by stating that?" Ricky wondered. He interjected before Monica could share her thoughts in response.

"So you think you could have killed Yolanda, Bootsy?" asked Ricky.

"It is what it is, bruh. I mean, anyone who gets in the way of us making progress out here in this jungle of criminal activity is a potential enemy. I'm just keeping it real—"

Ricky cut Bootsy off, in a hostile manner.

"Man, just give me a straight answer. Do-You-Think-You-Could-Have-Killed-Yolanda? That's all I want to know!"

Bootsy hesitated slightly in answering his ace. The last thing he wanted was for them to be at war. It would only signal division and Bootsy was well aware that a house divided couldn't stand. So he dropped back in his seat. That's when Monica interrupted.

"It doesn't matter!" she shouted.

"It does matter, Monica!"

"It doesn't! Just take me home, a'ight? 'Cause what's done is done and talking 'bout it ain't gonna bring her back."

"Wait, Monica, wait," said Bootsy nonchalantly as he sat back up. "Ricky asked me a question and I feel it's only right that I give him an answer."

Monica threw up both her hands reluctantly and allowed them to have it their way. "Look, Ricky," said Bootsy. "I'm gonna be straight with you, no bullshit. Yeah, I could have taken Yolanda out, if that's what the occasion called for."

"If that's what the occasion called for? Man, Yolanda was like family, to say the least. The occasion didn't call for that shit!" shouted Ricky.

"But that's your opinion, bruh!"

"No! That's not just my opinion," Ricky shouted. "That's a fact, dawg! Yolanda has always had all of our best interests at heart. You mean to tell me one slip up on her behalf and the damn death penalty becomes her reward? C'mon, let's be for real."

"Well, hell, bruh, what would you have done in the situation? Or shall I say it's already obvious?" asked Bootsy.

Ricky gripped his steering wheel tightly and clamped his teeth together in anger and disappointment. As he did so, silence filled the car. So much so, that if a mouse had been inside with a full bladder and unable to hold it, it could have been heard urinating on the carpet of the Cadillac's floorboard.

******

The eyes of both Bootsy and Monica were fixed hard on Ricky at this point of his madness, but Ricky didn't care. Hiding what he felt wasn't an option. For he loved Yolanda. Ricky loved her more than he had ever expressed while she was alive. He knew fully well from being around Yolanda long enough, that she did indeed have a big mouth. But Ricky also knew that she wouldn't run it and cause Monica, Bootsy, or him any harm intentionally. *How could Monica have done this to her?* Ricky wondered. *And how could Bootsy even say that under the circumstances, he would have done the same?* Those responses from Monica and Bootsy baffled Ricky. There was just no way he could see himself taking Yolanda's life, under any circumstances.

He thought on the matter for a few minutes before saying another word. Ricky shook his head from left to right slowly, while thinking. Sadness flooded his heart, causing tears to fall from his eyes without restraint. Tears that Monica clearly saw and moved to wipe away while Bootsy looked on. But Ricky turned away, indicating to Monica in no uncertain terms that now was not the time to touch him. Especially not with the hands she had used to put his sweetheart to death.

Ricky remained silent, like a hardened criminal under arrest. He was determined to keep it that way until he was somehow able to get past what he was feeling inside.

But Bootsy, Ricky's number one ace, insisted that he give an answer without delay.

******

"So, Ricky, bruh, what would you have done?" asked Boosty a second time, as if Ricky didn't hear him the first time.

Unable to tolerate Bootsy's impatience, Ricky hastily pulled his car over to the side of the road. He hit his brakes hard, causing nearly everything inside that wasn't bolted down tightly to propel forward, Monica and Bootsy included. Immediately thereafter, Ricky turned around to face Bootsy.

"You wanna know what the fuck I would've done, dawg? You really wanna know?"

Even though Bootsy was almost upset at Ricky for hitting his brakes so hard, he affirmed Ricky's question by nodding his head.

Ricky gave it to him raw. "Dawg, I would have utterly disfigured that bitch ass nigga who robbed Monica and cut off Ali's finger. But I think you know that already! And regarding Yolanda, yeah, I would have spanked her lil ass for slipping up and bringing all of this drama about. Killing her though, would have been out of the question. I just don't agree with that decision."

Ricky took his focus off Bootsy and shifted it toward Monica. "Furthermore, what puzzles me is why Bootsy and I were left in the blind about what was about to fuckin' go down. Shit, we're the enforcers of this click of ours, right?"

Directly upon hearing Ricky shout at her, Monica jumped out of the car in a rage and stood a few feet from the passenger door. She left the door swinging wide open while she pulled her gun out and positioned it to her head.

Death, No Exceptions!

What the fuck is Monica doing? Bootsy asked himself. Then he heard Monica shouting.

"Ricky, I will pull this muthafuckin' trigger if you don't just take me the fuck home! It's been a long ass two days for me and I don't wanna hear anymore about the situation."

Ricky took a deep breath and leaned sideways in Monica's direction. He reached out his hand as far as he could. "Give me the gun, Monica, and get back into the car, will you? Shit, people are already slowing down and looking over at us. One of 'em bound to call the police!"

"I don't give a fuck! Damn them!" shouted Monica as she removed the gun from her head only to begin waving it at onlookers. She aimed the gun at one onlooker. "You wanna get shot, muthafucka?" The onlooker sped off, nearly running into someone. That's when Bootsy stepped out. He knew that if he didn't do something they'd all be going to jail soon. So he approached her with caution. "Please, Monica. Please get in the car."

Monica stood there, numb. Bootsy placed one hand gently at her side while he reached for her gun with his other hand. Reluctantly, she handed over her gun. Afterward, she nearly fell into his arms crying. "It's okay, Monica. It's okay. That whole situation is over, like you said. We're taking you home now."

Both of them got back into the car. This time though, Monica got into the back seat with Bootsy. She placed her head in his lap and cried the whole way home.

CHAPTER SIXTEEN
William

Fearing choking to death, William knew that he had to get himself up and out of Yolanda's burning apartment before fire personnel and police arrived. He had played possum long enough.

He made his way to his feet, holding the base of his bloody neck where the bullet from Monica's gun had deeply grazed him. William saw Yolanda's body laid out on the floor. She was as dead as a tooth without nerves, but he dared not feel overly bad about her current state. He knew all too well that the same fate would have been his had it not been for quick thinking and a bit of theatrics.

As he stumbled toward the living room, coughing like a man with chronic bronchitis, he found himself prohibited from making an exit in that direction due to the blazing flames. The living room was where his attempted killer had ignited the fire. He quickly u-turned. Not without problems, though. The thickness of the black smoke made it difficult for him to see, let alone breathe. The only exit route he found was through a window in Yolanda's bedroom and he took it without question, climbing out headfirst as he inhaled and exhaled profusely.

William lay on the ground a moment, letting the fresh oxygen permeate his body. But while he was doing so, a neighbor who had phoned 911 after she heard Yolanda's fire alarm constantly going off, walked up. "Sir, are you okay?" she asked.

When William heard her voice, he jumped up, frightening the neighbor, and made a Carl Lewis run for it until he felt he was no longer in anyone's sight.

Without being spotted, William quickly ran to the nearest payphone and called Emily, but he received no answer. He kept trying, but to no avail. Figuring Emily was probably in a deep sleep, he phoned for a taxi to her place.

Luckily, he had a key, because once he arrived and entered Emily's crib, he discovered that she was not in a deep sleep as he had previously assumed.

She was, in fact, gone. And so was Rachael. A brief note was posted on the face of Emily's television. The note read:

William, I have left. I am headed to Savannah to take Rachael home. I will be back by late this evening, so stick around because I got something very important to kick it with you about.

And, oh, by the way, JD called me about an hour after you had left. He wanted three more of them "thangs" for a friend of his. You only had two left. I hit him off with that. Check under my mattress for the loot! See you when I get back.

After reading Emily's note, William went into her bedroom to retrieve some fresh clothes from her closet. He grabbed one of the brand new Nike outfits Emily had bought him from the mall, along with new Nike tennis shoes. Then he threw off the clothes and shoes that he had on. He placed them in Emily's trashcan with the intent of never putting them on again. He wanted nothing that reminded him of the near death experience he'd just encountered. The scenery that was locked in his mind, along with the scar on his neck, were sufficient enough as a reminder. He went and took a shower.

He stayed in the shower at least ten minutes before getting out. As he dried himself off and put a band aid on his neck, lotioned himself down, he took a long look at himself in the mirror and shook his head. "I'm supposed to be dead as a muthafucka," he said aloud to himself. He continued talking to himself as he walked back into Emily's bedroom to put on his clothes. "I knew I shouldn't have trusted that damn bitch, Yolanda, from the start. Callin' me out the blue, talkin' 'bout she just had me on her mind. That bitch planned my demise, like it was my fault that her sexy ass friend, Monica, got caught slippin'. I got something for that damn Monica, though. I got something for her ass."

William cut his conversation with himself short after hearing the phone ring. He got up to answer it. But at the moment he was about to pick up the receiver, he said, "Fuck it," and decided to look under Emily's mattress. He discovered the cash from Emily's sale of his coke. He thought it would be better to count the cash, than chat with whoever it was trying to call in.

******

Ricky remained in the car while Bootsy escorted a distraught Monica inside her condo. All Ricky could seem to think about while awaiting Bootsy's return was Yolanda, Yolanda, Yolanda, and the fifth of Gin he had in the trunk of his car. He got out to retrieve it and then jumped back inside. He drank some of it in hopes of drowning the painful thoughts he was having of Yolanda's demise. He wondered if Yolanda died fast or was her death slow and painful. He knew Monica must've shot her. But how many times and where, was a mystery to him.

Sensing that Monica totally misunderstood where he was coming from with his opinion and view of the situation, he sought to get out of the car to have a talk with her. But when he glanced through his windshield at Monica's front door, which was open, he saw her and Bootsy conversing, hard. Bootsy was even holding one of Monica's hands in an intimate embrace. This sight left Ricky feeling somewhat jealous and left out. So he rethought going inside. Instead, he took a few more sips. And after more time had passed then he'd been keeping count of, he looked up and realized that Monica's front door was now closed. That's when he threw his car in reverse and skidded out of the driveway.

******

Monica and Bootsy's conversation was interrupted when both of them heard tires burning rubber. Bootsy looked outside and saw that it was Ricky. "Damn it, man! What the hell is wrong with Ricky?"

"What? Did he leave?" asked Monica.

"Damn right, he left. Shit!"

Ricky just up and leaving frustrated Bootsy to the point of him being upset at his ace. They had come together and, like always, they were supposed to leave together.

Monica, however, just sucked her teeth and waved it off. She headed upstairs to bathe. On the way up, she hollered down at Bootsy. "You can crash on the sofa if you want. Or you can grab the keys to my Benz and check up on Ricky. It's your choice. I'm definitely not about to let how he's feeling beat me down."

Bootsy dropped down hard on the sofa. He placed his hands on his head and sat there for about ten minutes. He reflected on the fact that he had been trying his best to comfort Monica, so that she wouldn't have a nervous breakdown or worse, commit suicide. So far, so good. All Monica needed was a little understanding from her partners about her disposition, which Bootsy was all too aware of. Because unlike he and Ricky, Monica wasn't from the hardcore streets. She had only inherited certain aspects of its behavior from her son's father, big Jay-Jay. And although she had squeezed that trigger a few times and killed, she definitely was not a killer. She was just a victim of being caught up in the moment of what she assumed he and Ricky would do in the situation she was placed in. *Why couldn't Ricky just understand that and keep what he was really feeling on ice, instead of outright being critical of the decision she'd made?* Bootsy pondered.

However the pie was sliced, one thing was certain in his mind. At the moment, he had to get up and check on his brother. And that's exactly what he did, without any further thought on the matter.

While upstairs, Monica took two barbiturate tablets to help induce sleep right before she got into the tub to bathe. As she was bathing, she began humming the tune, "Tracks of My Tears" by Motown's great, Smokey Robinson to keep her mind from taking her back to what she had done to William and Yolanda.

When she finished, she went into her bedroom, jumped into comfortable socks, panties and a T-shirt, and went to bed.

******

CHAPTER SEVENTEEN
Sir, Have You Been Drinking?

Ricky was on his way to Yolanda's apartment. By then it was a little after six in the morning, but he just had to see if what Monica had alleged she did was actually the truth.

As Ricky got closer to Yolanda's apartment, he indeed noticed from not so far away that her place had been nearly burned down. He also noticed a gang of cop cars in the area.

To his dismay, one of them got behind him and pulled him over.

"Look at this muthafuckin' shit!" he shouted out loud to himself. The police officer stepped out of his patrol car, walked up to Ricky's door, and greeted him.

"Good morning, sir. I pulled you over because I noticed you were swerving. I'm gonna need to see your driver's license."

"Swerving?" replied Ricky. "Officer, I don't know about all that, but ah here's my license." Ricky patted both his pockets before realizing that his license was in his sun visor. "Oh, here you go." He handed the officer his license. When the officer grabbed it from him, he noticed that Ricky's hand was shaking slightly and a strong aroma of alcohol was coming from the car.

"Excuse me, sir. Have you been drinking?"

"A little, Officer."

That answer alone gave the officer probable cause to suspect Ricky of drinking while under the influence.

"What would you call a little?" asked the officer.

"Hell, I don't know. Two or three drinks, maybe."

"Well, I tell you what, I'ma need you to step out cha vehicle and take a breathalyzer."

Ricky turned his head away from the officer and took a deep breath. "C'mon now, Officer. Is that really necessary? Hell, I'm just trying to make it home, that's all. Why you gotta be fuckin' wit' me? It's because I'm black, ain't it? Y'all white officers always pulling us young black guys over, man. Shit!"

"Look, Mr. Blakely, your race doesn't have a thing to do with this. My wife is a woman of color and I love her and her side of the family. So don't go trying to pull that race stuff on me. Besides, this is standard procedure. I'm just doing my job. Now, are you going step out of your car, or am I going to have to call for back up?"

Ricky paused a moment and took a deep breath. He was thinking about "flooring" it. His only problem was, the officer had his driver's license and if he floored it, it wouldn't be long before a warrant would be issued for his arrest. Plus, Ricky doubted he'd get far anyway, with all of the patrol cars concentrated in that area. So he went ahead and stepped out.

"I'm going to need you to turn around and put your hands behind your back."

"Officer, sir, am I under arrest?"

"No, sir, you're not. I just have to do this for my own safety."

"Do what you gotta do then," Ricky said.

As the officer was cuffing him, he peeked over Ricky's shoulder and inside the car, where a fifth of Gin was lying on the floorboard. It looked as if the bottle had been almost completely consumed. The officer escorted

Ricky to the backseat of his patrol car. "Just hang tight here for a minute."

The officer headed back to Ricky's car to search it. He retrieved the nearly empty bottle of Gin, and while he did that, something else grabbed his attention. On the same floorboard, underneath the driver's seat, was a large, see-through Ziploc bag. It didn't take the officer long to discover what was inside the bag—bundles of rubber band wrapped cash. The officer knew from working on the police force for the past fourteen years that only drug dealers carried cash wrapped that way.

He continued his search, figuring Ricky had to be a drug dealer, but he didn't find any drugs. What he did find, however, was something that guaranteed Ricky a trip to jail; a fully loaded .9mm Glock. Bootsy had left it in the backseat without Ricky's knowledge.

The officer walked back to his patrol car with everything that he had discovered in his hands. He held the money and the gun up for Ricky to see.

"You want to explain this?"

Ricky sucked his teeth and said, "Man, I ain't got no rap for you. C'mon and take me to jail."

"You sure you don't want to talk to me? I can hook you up with the right people to get you a deal, 'cause you're definitely facing prison time for being in possession of this gun."

"I ain't no rat, Officer, take me to jail. That's all I gotta say on the matter."

"You, betcha, young man."

******

Bootsy rode all over the city looking for his ace. He even stopped through Snaggle Cat's neighborhood. But he didn't spot Ricky's Cadillac in the driveway, where it would normally be parked, so he didn't bother going inside. The only area Bootsy didn't dare to look for Ricky was in Yolanda's neighborhood. Had he done so, he would more than likely have spotted the tow truck hauling Ricky's Cadillac to a designated location.

After the search for his ace proved fruitless, Bootsy headed back to Monica's crib. She was dead asleep and he didn't bother to wake her to tell her that he couldn't find Ricky. Monica's night and morning had been long and stressful enough already. Therefore, he allowed her to enjoy her rest while he crashed on the sofa.

Getting some sleep was his chief mission at the moment, but constant thoughts of his ace's whereabouts plagued him, causing him to become restless. He grabbed the remote, turned on the television and flipped through the channels. He landed on the news channel, after spotting what looked like Yolanda's neighborhood in the scenery behind the reporter. In the top right hand corner of the screen were the words, "Previously Recorded." Bootsy turned up the volume and began listening to what the reporter had to say.

Authorities for the Charlotte Police Department say that they were called to this now burned down apartment when a neighbor heard a fire alarm going off sometime early this morning. When firefighters arrived, they discovered a badly decomposed female body. Police say they don't know much about the woman. A neighbor, however, ID'd her as the occupant of the apartment. The neighbor identified the woman as Yolanda Owens.

The neighbor also told police that she witnessed a suspicious looking black male escaping from a bedroom window. Police detectives are not sure if this black male is directly responsible for the fire. Detectives say they would like to speak with this individual and they are asking that anyone with any information regarding this incident contact Detective

Robert Blame at 704-231-8981. Detectives say your identity will remain anonymous.

Bootsy turned off the television and said, "Oh shit! That muthafucka still alive!"

He got up from the sofa and went into the bathroom, where he washed his face with cold water to refresh himself. Then he grabbed the keys to Monica's Benz and stormed out of her condo.

******

Bootsy drove to Yolanda's apartment. The scenery was just as he had seen on television, complete with yellow crime scene tape. He got out of the car and went next door to speak with the neighbor the reported had mentioned on television. He knocked at her door and not long afterward he heard a female voice say, "Who is it?"

"Bootsy. I'm a friend of Yolanda's."

The neighbor opened the door. "Can I help you with something?"

"Yes, I'm a friend of Yolanda's, and I was wondering if you could fill me in on what happened over at her place."

"Well, to be honest with you one of the police detectives told me not to say anything about what I saw to anyone but them, so—"

Bootsy cut her off. "So, please let me come inside, if you don't mind."

Before she could invite Bootsy inside, he walked in. "I'm not trying to be rude or anything, Miss, but Yolanda was like my sister. I gotta know what happened to her."

Just as Bootsy said that, a little girl who looked to be about eleven years old came into the living room.

"Momma, who is that?"

"Don't worry about it. What I tell you 'bout being so nosy? Go on back in your room."

The little girl went back into her room.

"Kids are so damn nosy these days. Excuse me."

"That's okay."

"Like I was saying, the police detectives told me not to—"

Again, Bootsy cut her off. This time, however, he pulled a wad of cash from his pocket—at least three or four thousand dollars. He placed it on the table near him. "Miss, do you wanna talk to me for some paper, or do you want to hold what you know for the police? It's up to you. Like I said, I just want to know what happened to my sister."

The neighbor quickly changed her mind about holding back and told Bootsy what she'd seen.

"All I can tell you is that I am the one who called 911 after I heard Yolanda's fire alarm constantly going off. Not long afterward, I saw a slender black guy climbing out of her window. He was wearing a T-shirt and sweat pants, and his neck was bloody. I offered to help him, but the moment he saw me he ran and didn't look back."

"You ever seen him over here with Yolanda before?"

"I don't recall. I just know his behavior was really suspicious, like he didn't wanna be spotted. I sure hate that happened to Yolanda. God knows I do."

Bootsy stared off into space for a moment. For the first time since he had heard about what actually happened to Yolanda from Monica, his eyes began to water.

"Would you like some coffee or something to drink?" asked the neighbor.

"No, no, no. I gotta be leaving now. I appreciate everything."

The woman looked at the wad of cash Bootsy had given her and said, "No problem."

"Don't spend all that in one place, and buy that pretty little girl of yours something nice."

Bootsy jumped back into Monica's Benz and rolled out.

"That black muthafucka still alive. How in the hell could that be?" he contemplated on his way back to Monica's condo. "How in the hell could that be?"

CHAPTER EIGHTEEN
Snaggle Cat

Monica's telephone line had a busy signal, which annoyed Ricky every time he tried her number. He needed to get in touch with her and Bootsy bad as hell, to alert them about his current situation. His bond had been set at $50,000. However, $5,000 would get him out with Daniel's Bondsmen Company. The money wasn't a problem. Ricky had plenty of that stashed away for a rainy day such as this. He kept trying Monica's number, but still received a busy signal, so he decided to call Snaggle Cat.

She answered on the first ring. "Hello?"

"Snaggle Cat?"

"Yes, dis me."

"Ah, this Ricky. I been arrested—"

"Arrested?" Snaggle Cat said, cutting him off.

"Yeah. I'm in the county jail and it doesn't look good. The damn police took $13,500 out my car. Plus, a fully loaded .9mm. They also charged me with DWI."

"What's your bail?"

"Fifty..."

"Fifty dollars?"

"Fuck no, Snaggle Cat! Fifty fuckin' thousand!"

"Damn, why the hell is it so high?"

"Because the bitch ass policeman who arrested me told the judge that I had been an asshole with him, and that he suspected that I was a big drug dealer."

"Shit, that ain't nothing but fuckin' mere suspicion—"

"I know, Snaggle Cat, I know. I'm contacting my lawyer first thing Monday morning about it. The cop didn't have a search warrant to search my car. Anyway, look here, I need you."

"Anything for you, Ricky. You know that. What's up?"

"I need you to go upstairs and look in the first closet on your left hand side, the one right before you get to your bedroom."

"I know the one you're talking 'bout."

"Well, look on the top shelf to the right, under those clothes, and you will find a black shoebox. Get $5,000 out of it and take it down to Daniel's Bondsmen Company. Ask for Eric. They call him Big E. Tell him you're there on my behalf."

"I'll get right on it, right now. I promise."

"Bet," Ricky said before hanging up.

******

Snaggle Cat retrieved the bail money and did what Ricky had requested of her. A few hours later, she and Big E bailed Ricky out with no problem.

When Ricky got out, he was so glad to see Snaggle Cat and know that she could be relied on, he hugged her, smacked her hard on her butt, and said, "That's *my* girl!" Then Ricky looked over at Big E and gave him a high-five. "Thanks, dawg. You know I appreciate it."

"I know you do, playa. You shoulda had her call me first and I would have come and got you, and picked up the money later. Hell, I know you stand by your word."

"I wasn't even thinking, man. Thanks again though, dawg."

Ricky threw his arm around Snaggle Cat's neck and said, "Let's get up out of here."

Snaggle Cat put her arm around Ricky's waist and looked up at him, grinning. "Thought I wasn't gonna do what you asked me, didn't you? I know you did."

"Nah, you and I been riding together too long for me to start second guessing you. I trust you, big girl. You my baby."

When Ricky said that, Snaggle Cat tightened her grip on his waist.

She appreciated him saying that. It made her feel like Ricky didn't just see her as a crack cocaine addict who should be mistreated and unworthy of trust. His words made her feel like she was family, which was major. In this cold world, where nearly anything went on, family was all you had to rely on.

As she, Ricky and Big E exited the county jail, Big E's pager went off, so he had to go his own way. "I'ma holler at cha, Ricky," Big E said before splitting company with them.

"A'ight, dawg. I'll hollar at cha," replied Ricky.

"You know, Rick," Snaggle Cat said as the two of them waited for their taxi to arrive, "I'm about to stop using cocaine."

"For real, Snaggle Cat?"

"For real, Ricky. And I'm serious this time."

"What made you all of a sudden get serious about that?"

"I don't know. I guess I'm just starting to realize that there's more to life than constantly getting high on a daily basis. I mean, shit, look at me; I'm not getting any younger. Life is fuckin' passing me by. I just feel it's time for me to get it together."

"It's kinda strange that you said that, 'cause, believe it or not, while I was sitting in that holding cell waiting on you to come get me, I was thinking to myself that it's time for me to stop selling drugs. Hell, I got enough money stashed away—"

"You damn sho do," Snaggle Cat said. "I saw a lot of it."

"Yeah, but what you saw wasn't really nothing, Snaggle Cat. I got more elsewhere.

Not only that, but something tragic happened to someone I really loved very early this morning, and when I heard about it, it was like a dagger had been thrust into my heart." Ricky's eyes began to water.

Snaggle Cat had never seen him behave this way. She knew whatever had happened had to be serious.

"Whatever it is, Ricky," Snaggle Cat said, rubbing her hand up and down his back, "it'll be okay. Storms only last for a season."

Ricky fought back his tears, and even though he wanted desperately to talk about the root cause of his sadness and grief, he fought that, as well. "It's just, one minute you think everything is going fine in your life, then BOOM life throws you a curve ball."

Snaggle Cat spotted the taxi approaching from a distance. It was held up at a traffic light. "Yeah Ricky, I know all about curve balls. What I have learned from them is that we don't have to allow them to strike us out. Even curve balls can be hit out of the park for a home run, depending on who's at bat. With the heart and mind that I know is within you, you can turn any tragedy into a triumph."

Ricky looked at Snaggle Cat as if surprised to hear her encourage him as she did. "Girl, you gon' make me love you!"

Snaggle Cat smiled, and then lifted her hand to flag down the taxi driver.

******

Bootsy didn't know whether to awaken Monica or let her sleep. He paced the floor, thinking on the matter. The way he figured, if this cat, William, had caught Monica slippin' once already and robbed her of her coke, her loot, and her son's limb, there was no question that if he caught up with her now it would be death, no exceptions for her.

"Fuck it," Bootsy said to himself. "I gotta tell her!"

Bootsy headed upstairs to wake Monica, but before he could get midway up the stairs his pager went off. He stopped to check it and discovered that it was Ricky. He headed back down the stairs to the living room phone, where he found it impossible to dial out due to Monica's bedroom phone being off the hook. He ran upstairs to hang up her phone.

While in her bedroom, Bootsy saw that Monica was still in a deep sleep. He grabbed her phone and called Ricky.

Snaggle Cat's phone rang three times before Ricky answered. "Yo, what's up?"

"Ricky, what's up, bruh? Where you at?" asked Bootsy. "I been looking all over for your ass."

"You don't recognize this number, dawg? I'm at Snaggle Cat's place."

"I was so in a hurry to call you back, I wasn't paying attention. I drove over that way earlier though, and didn't spot your Cadillac."

"Man, dawg, I'm 'bout to tell you why you didn't spot my Caddy and you ain't gon' believe it. First, let me apologize for leaving you and Monica. I shouldn't have done that."

"I ain't trippin', man. As long as you alright."

"Check this out, though. When I left you and Monica, I headed to Yolanda's neighborhood, dawg. I just had to see for myself if Monica had in fact did what she told us she did. Well, sure enough, she wasn't lying, cause from what I saw, Yolanda's apartment was nearly burned to the ground. Making a long story short, when I was in that area, the damn police got behind me and pulled me over. The muthafucka illegally searched my fuckin' car and found $13,500, and your fully-loaded .9mm in the backseat."

"Damn, dawg, my bad. I forgot I left it."

"It ain't no problem. The police also charged me with DWI. Out of all of those charges, that's the only one that's gonna stick. So now I got a case. But like I said, the cop searched my damn car without a search warrant."

"Who bailed you out?"

"Snaggle Cat and Big E came and got me. I tried calling y'all, but I kept getting a fuckin' busy signal."

"Monica had the phone off the hook, unbeknownst to me."

"Where is she?"

"She's right here, sleeping like a bear in hibernation. Listen." Bootsy put the phone to Monica's mouth so Ricky could hear her snoring. "You heard her?"

"Yeah. She's knocked the fuck out, isn't she?"

"I was 'bout to wake her up, 'cause, bruh, we all need to talk."

"Oh, I know we do. We all need to talk badly."

"Nah, bruh, this ain't about what you may think you know. It's something else a little more serious."

"Well, talk to me, Bootsy. Fill in the blanks for me. What's up?"

"I'll share it with you and Monica when you get here. It's just that serious."

"I gotta go and pick up my car first, 'cause you know they towed it. But I'll be right over there afterward."

"See you when you get here. Be careful."

"Bet."

CHAPTER NINETEEN
Time for a Change

William had devised a plan while he was counting his cash. He had determined that he was gonna get a gun and stake out Monica. At the right time, he would surprise her with one to the temple. After all, she did try to take his life without compromise.

However, in the midst of his thought process, something happened that aided him in reconsidering his plan.

It was early Sunday morning and nearly every radio station was playing gospel music or airing a sermon. Normally, William preferred listening to the music, even though it was gospel, but there was something about one preacher's sermon that made William give it his undivided attention. The preacher said, "What would it profit a man if he gains the whole world and loses his soul?"

How can a man lose his soul, William thought? The preacher went on to explain as if actually hearing William's question. "The soul of a man is the life force that God breathes into man for him or her to exemplify a godly life and character, while living on this earth. But in today's world, you don't see much godliness, now do you?"

"No, sir, you don't, Pastor," William heard the congregation say in the background.

The pastor continued. "You don't see much godliness, because individuals have lost their souls. Yes, they have lost that godly element that would keep their lives patterned after God's righteousness. Just look around you in this world. Somebody is always looking to snatch your pocketbook or your wallet, and if you're lucky or fortunate, you may walk away from such encounters alive. These soul-less thugs don't care a thing about taking other people's lives. They just don't care. I tell ya they need Jesus Christ to help them regain their life, because these soul-less individuals are walking dead!"

William hurried up and turned off the radio. He had heard enough. But what he couldn't turn off were the preacher's words. They seemed to be echoing loudly deep inside him. "These soul-less thugs don't care a thing about taking other people's lives."

He finished counting his money. Then he placed Emily's cut to the side and walked over to the mirror to examine his neck again. Auntie Pearl came close to losing me, he thought as he looked in the mirror. The reality of that hit him like a freight train. He knew that, had his Auntie Annie Pearl gotten news of him dying by way of violence, it would have undeniably broken her heart. This thought, coupled with what he had heard the preacher say, made William conclude that it was undoubtedly time for a change.

******

Monica finally rolled over from her deep sleep. She looked at the clock and saw that it was 4:15 p.m. She couldn't believe she had slept that late, but she was so glad that she had, despite knowing that she had to pick up Ali from her mother's place.

She got up and went into the bathroom to pee. Afterward, she headed downstairs for coffee, where she discovered Bootsy asleep on the sofa, with his mouth wide open. Monica went over and placed her hand underneath his chin. Her touch woke him immediately. "Close your mouth, boy. I could smell your breath all the way upstairs."

"Yeah, right, Monica. How long have you been up?" asked Bootsy.

"Not long. Ten, fifteen minutes, maybe."

"What time is it?"

"Close to five o'clock."

Bootsy sat up. "I finally talked to Ricky."

"Oh, yeah? You caught up with him, huh?"

"I didn't catch up with him, he paged me. How about he got locked up shortly after he left here?"

"What?"

"Yep. The police got behind him, searched the car, took a lot of cash, and took my .9mm Glock. He said they charged him with DWI, too. Snaggle Cat went and bailed him out after he couldn't reach us."

"Whatcha mean he couldn't reach us?"

"He said he kept getting a busy signal."

"Oh, snap! I forgot all about taking the phone off the hook. Shit, he gon' be mad as hell at me!"

"You might be right, Monica. I don't know. But he did apologize for leaving. He was supposed to be over here already."

"Well, you know him," said Monica as she walked into the kitchen. "You want some coffee?"

Bootsy got up and walked to the kitchen. He stood in the doorway. "Yeah, I'll take a cup. I need some energy right about now anyway."

"I bet you do, after rippin' and runnin', trying to find Ricky all morning. There's some pop tarts over there somewhere, if you want some to go with your coffee."

"Just coffee will be good. I got something I need to talk to you about," said Bootsy.

"What's that? Wait, grab you a cup from up there in that cabinet. This coffee is hot as hell."

Bootsy grabbed a cup. "You want one, too?"

"Yeah, hand me one."

Bootsy placed both cups next to the coffeemaker while Monica poured their coffee.

"Bootsy, if you don't mind, grab that sugar and creamer from out of the same cabinet."

"I gotcha." He retrieved the sugar and creamer, and placed them next to their cups. "I don't drink sugar or creamer in my coffee. I like mine black. "

"Cowboy style, huh?"

"Yeah, cowboy style."

"I hear ya, Mr. Tough Guy. I have to have at least some sugar in it. I like mine sweet."

"Sweet like you, right?"

"You crazy, boy. You know that? What you mean by that, anyway? 'Cause you know I can be sour as a lemon, too, sometimes. I think they call it bipolar?"

"We all got a little bipolar in us, depending on how hard the wind blows. But, for the most part, Monica, since I've known you, all I've seen in you is a sweet, nice, intelligent woman, who would probably give someone the shoes off her feet if that person needed them."

"Why, thank you, Bootsy. I appreciate you recognizing that in me," Monica replied, somewhat cutting him off. "Makes me feel like somebody's been paying me some attention. You know, Bootsy, women love attention. The right kind, that is."

"I pay attention to everything, Monica. E-ve-ry-thing," said Bootsy, licking his lips.

Monica blushed. "I assume that's a good thing," she replied before attempting to head back upstairs. Bootsy grabbed her arm gently and stopped her from going too far. Monica turned around and when she did, the two of them were so close their lips nearly touched. Bootsy looked in her eyes and licked his lips again.

"There's something I need to share with you without further procrastination. But to be completely honest with you, I don't know how to say this…"

Monica cut Bootsy off. "I already know. I already know you like me, Bootsy. Yolanda told me, so you can be straightforward, baby. Hell, it ain't like I'm Miss America."

"Monica, you're a thousand, upon a thousand Miss Americas, in my book. And that's just me keepin' it real."

Monica placed a hand on her hip and smirked, "Ummm, hmmm, I hear ya."

"Trust me; I wouldn't ever lie to you. No real man has to lie."

"Thank you. But as far as a relationship goes, you gotta give me some time. The damn flowers on Big Jay-Jay's grave haven't even begun to wither yet. It's just too early for me."

"I'm patient, trust me. However, that's not what I wanted to talk with you about."

"You better be kidding me, or I'm going upstairs to get my .38."

Before Bootsy could utter another word, the doorbell rang. "Here, hold my coffee for me, while I see who this is at my door."

******

"I'm gon' bust your ass, William," Emily shouted. She had just gotten back from Savannah, Georgia, and couldn't wait to tell William what was on her mind.

"What are you talking about?" asked William as they both kicked it in her bedroom.

"How about two o'clock this morning I heard Rachael talking in her damn sleep?"

"Okay. And..."

"And I heard her saying; please don't let my cousin find out that you had your dick in my mouth. She'll kill me."

William immediately burst out laughing. "The damn girl was dreaming, for heaven's sake! What are you getting all hysterical about?"

"I'm getting fuckin' hysterical because she didn't just say that, she actually described *it* as if she had actually had some of it. Now I know damn well you didn't fuck my cousin, did you?"

"Emily, come here, baby. Look at me." Emily looked William squarely in his eyes. "Baby," he said, holding both of her shoulders in his hands, "I did not fuck your cousin. I promise I didn't. Now, thank you for getting rid of that coke for us. That's right, *us*! Here's your cut. What's mine is yours, baby, and you know what," William got down on his knees. "Baby, you the only woman, besides my Auntie Pearl, whom I have ever trusted. I want you to marry me. I'm through with the streets. You see this on my neck? I gotta be honest with you. Earlier, I almost lost my life. Baby, I'm tired. Hell, enough is enough and enough is too much. I just wanna settle the fuck down. Marry me, Emily, will you?"

"That depends on how big the diamond in my ring is," replied Emily. "No, but for real, it depends on how much your ass is willing to stay out of the streets. I don't need a husband who is gonna spend more time in the streets than with me."

"Baby, I promise on the life of my auntie, and you know I love her, I'm finished with the streets. Finished!"

"You for real as hell, too, aren't you?"

"I'm for real as a heart attack! Baby, I promise."

"In that case the answer is YES!"

William jumped up and gave Emily the biggest tongue kiss he could manage. Then he said, "I promise I'll be a good husband."

CHAPTER TWENTY
Enough Damage Done

"Sorry about this morning," said Ricky, greeting Monica with a kiss and a bouquet of flowers as he stepped inside her living room.

"You don't have to mention it. Thanks for the flowers. They're beautiful."

"You're welcome." Ricky saw Bootsy coming into the living room with two cups in his hands.

"What up, bruh? See you finally made it over," shouted Bootsy before Ricky could say anything.

"Yeah, well, hell, I had to make a few moves," said Ricky.

Monica interjected. "Why did a taxi have to bring you here, Ricky?"

"Bootsy didn't tell you what happened to me this morning?"

"He told me, but did you leave something out, Bootsy?"

"I forgot to tell you his car got towed."

"So, what they gon' keep it?"

"I called down there and they gon' allow me to get it first thing Monday morning. It's cool. I'll be a'ight 'til then. So what was so important that you needed me to be over here in a hurry, Bootsy?"

Bootsy placed both cups of coffee on Monica's living room table.

"You might want me to set those flowers down for you, too, Monica."

Monica shook her head. "No, that's okay. I got 'em."

"Well, looka here. I got some bad news, y'all."

"Hell, that's all I been hearing anyway," said Ricky.

Monica looked over at him and rolled her eyes. "Please don't start."

Ricky threw up both of his hands.

"Yo, the bad news is that muthafucka is still alive."

Monica stared at Bootsy through squinted eyes. "Who?" Both she and Ricky shouted at the same time.

"The buster who robbed you, Monica. I saw it on the news this morning. He was seen by a neighbor climbing out of Yolanda's bedroom window."

"Fuck no! I don't believe that shit. I shot that muthafucka."

"I don't doubt you did, but somehow he survived."

"But how?"

"I have no idea."

"What about Yolanda?" asked Ricky.

"She's...she's gone, bruh."

Monica interjected, "I saw that dude laid out on the floor. How could he be alive?"

"Like I said, I don't know. But he is alive, apparently. He was wounded though, because after I saw it on the news, rather than wake you from your sleep, I drove over there and spoke with the neighbor. She told me that she saw him holding his neck, which looked to her to be bloody. So with this dude still being alive, looks like we may be back at square one."

"That's if the muthafucka didn't run somewhere and collapse from bleeding the fuck to death. That's why we should have been called to handle that pussy ass nigga in the first place!" said Ricky.

"I said, don't start, Ricky," shouted Monica.

"Don't get me wrong, sis. I didn't say that to belittle you. But Monica, let's keep it real now, certain jobs are for certain people. I mean, with all due respect, you're not a violent person. C'mon now, I'm not stupid."

"What are you saying, I am?"

"Hell-to-the-no, so stop taking every little thing so damn personally, will you?"

"I hear you, Ricky, but for the record let me get this out right now. I want you and Bootsy to know that it was my intention to contact y'all as soon as I found out about Yolanda knowing this dude. It was Yolanda who told me not to notify y'all.

"She told me that she was gonna set the dude up by convincing him to come over to her crib. While he was there and relaxed, she told me that I should come out with my gun and surprise him, so that's what happened. And that's the real reason I didn't contact y'all. I put that on the life of my son."

Ricky looked over at Bootsy and took a deep breath. He didn't doubt one word Monica said. But since Yolanda wasn't present to defend herself against these allegations, he just threw his hands up and said, "Fuck it!"

Bootsy added to it. "Yeah, fuck it. What's done is done. Now it's time to do whatever else we gotta do and find this dude."

"Only this time, Monica," said Ricky, "if we run into him, let me and Bootsy handle it, a'ight?"

"No problem, bruh. Y'all got that," replied Monica.

"Furthermore, I want to say this. When we finish getting rid of the coke we got left, I'm through hustling. This shit ain't fun for me anymore. Shit, it's time to experience something new. Hell, we all got money put up and Monica you majored in business in college. Let's come up with something and let's all go legit, before we end up losing every fuckin' thing."

Bootsy agreed and so did Monica.

Then Ricky stretched out his hand. "Come touch my hand, Bootsy, and you, too, Monica." Bootsy's hand landed on top of Ricky's and Monica's hand landed on top of Bootsy's. "Look, we are a family and we must remain solid and loyal in order for the family to survive. There are no big I's or little u's, there's only us, the family. Anything else outside of that is a violation of our unity. Do you agree?" Both Monica and Bootsy agreed.

Afterward, they showed one another love with hugs and kisses.

******

(Two Days Later)

Monica was sitting on her front steps, playing with little Ali and having a conversation with her neighbor, Mrs. Rose, when she received mail straight from the hands of the mailman. The mailman delivered Mrs. Rose's mail, too.

Mrs. Rose looked through hers briefly. "Bills, bills, and more bills," she said, before telling Monica that she'd talk with her later.

When Mrs. Rose went back into her condo, Monica grabbed Ali by the hand and went inside her own condo. There, Monica looked through her mail. She noticed an envelope with an inscription on it that read: "It Wasn't All Her Fault, Neither Was It All Mine." The envelope didn't have a return address on it, which made Monica curious all the more to open it and review its contents. She sat Ali down next to her on her couch, opened the envelope and started reading the letter she found inside.

******

Dear Monica,

I hope this letter reaches you with an open mind. I am writing you because I felt it necessary to shoot at you with the truth and not with bullets. Trust me though, it took an act of God and me using my head for me to come to this point, which I hope will ultimately benefit us both. My initial natural reaction was to do unto you what you attempted to do unto me. The only difference being, I was gonna make sure you were a dead woman, no exceptions! After all, you really did intend to kill me. I saw it in your eyes.

However, I want you to know that, although it may be impossible for you to forgive me for what I did to your son, I do apologize to you for that. It was never my intention to hurt or harm him, God as my witness. I only put my straight razor to his neck in an attempt to get you to respond to my demands truthfully.

Unfortunately, you held back on me. How? Well, remember when I asked you where you were hiding the coke and cash? Your response was, "What coke and cash?" That response made me feel like you were trying to play me for a sucker, and I didn't wait for you in the parking lot of that daycare center to be played like a sucker.

I knew from what Yolanda shared with me when she was drunk, that you did, in fact, have what I was demanding of you. One thing I knew from dealing with Yolanda was that she wouldn't lie to me without good reason. Anyway, since you insisted on playing senile on me, I had to hurt what you loved most—your child—because the way I figured it, no true mother in her right mind would sacrifice her child for the sake of guarding something so material as coke and cash. I had hoped you saw it that way, also, but I was wrong, and your son lost a portion of his finger as a result.

After I finally showed you that I was serious, you decided to cooperate with me. Why couldn't you cooperate with me from the beginning, Monica? Everything would have gone just fine.

Moreover, let me say this: Killing your best friend wasn't at all justifiable. That girl loved you. Everything I ever heard her say about you was good. She even referred to you as the only sister she ever had. She said that the two of you had known each other ever since y'all were kids, and that she was so sorry you lost your son's father because of a drug deal that had gone bad, or something like that.

When she was telling me about you, she had no idea that I would later plot to rob you. I gave her no indication of that at all. The only thing she can be faulted for is inadvertently hipping me to you, which, as she said before you shot her in cold blood, was an honest mistake.

Certainly, Monica, we all make 'em. I know I have. I've made plenty of mistakes. But now, after surviving your attempt to kill me, I have come to the conclusion that enough is enough. That maybe God is trying to tell me something. That is why I have decided not to retaliate and trust me, I certainly could have. Yesterday, I rode through your neighborhood and I spotted you, your son, and two other guys. I could have done something very, very vicious, but I swallowed my pride, like the woman who raised me taught me to do when I have been offended. Don't get me wrong, I'm not a saint. I'm just tired of being stupid.

I'm gonna end this letter now, but I can assure you that you don't have to worry about me creeping up on you to hurt or harm you. Matter of fact, I'm not even gonna be in the city, 'cause it's like this in my view—God spared my life for a reason. Now, I must move forward to see what that reason is.

So, again, I apologize for what happened to your son. Just keepin' it real.

"A Survivor"

******

Monica was rendered speechless after reading the letter. So were Bootsy and Ricky, whom she called hours later and showed it to. In spite of William's apology and overall view of the matter, Bootsy and Ricky both harmonized in their desire to find and kill him. But Monica, after giving it much thought, persuaded them to do otherwise.

"Let him go," she said. "Let him go. It's over. It's time for us to do as you made mention of the other day, Ricky. It's time for the three of us to go legit. Monica motioned for little Ali to come to her. He was sitting on Bootsy's lap.

Bootsy lifted Ali and set him on his feet. "Go to Momma," he said.

Ali walked to Monica and she picked him up. "Enough damage done. I can't afford to lose everything. None of us can. It's over."

******

Ricky walked over to a framed picture that Monica had in her living room, on top of her 54-inch floor model television. The picture was of Monica and Yolanda in the club, sitting at a table, toasting drinks in their hands. Both of them were cheesing hard. Ricky purposely blocked Monica out of the picture and focused strictly on Yolanda. He picked the picture frame up and looked at it hard, taking note of every single detail. Monica and Bootsy, along with little Ali, had gone upstairs. *I swear before heaven and earth that I will never let it go, Yolanda. I'm gonna make it my goddamn business to get that nigga. Therefore, sweetheart, it ain't over till it's over. And I mean that fuckin' shit...*

He then saw Bootsy making his way back down the stairs.

"You ready to bounce, my nigga?" Bootsy asked, with the keys to Monica's Benz in his hands.

"Yeah. But shit, what you gon' follow behind me in Monica's car? I see you got her keys..."

"Nah, she just told me to leave them on top of the television."

"Let's roll then," said Ricky. "I got something real important to take care of anyway."

Chapter Twenty One
[It Ain't Over]

The moment Ricky and Bootsy exited Monica's driveway, Ricky looked over at Bootsy and said, "Dawg, for real, if you think for one moment that I'm gonna let that nigga get away with what he did to little Ali, then you out of all people don't know me at all."

"Ricky, that's not really the issue. The issue is Monica. She wants out of this shit. You know, the game. What she did to Yolanda is killing the fuck out of her.

She been acting strange and shit ever since. That shit fuckin' wit' her."

"Look, dawg, she can get out of the game all she wants. I ain't mad at her. All I'm fuckin' saying is, it ain't over by a long shot."

"Bruh, I feel the same way. I mean, reading that muthafuckin' letter that nigga sent to Monica was something. The nigga said he could have gotten us all. Shit!

Ain't no enemy like the one you can't see, but can see you. You feel me—"

"The nigga should have did what he had to do and put a hole in my head," Ricky said, cutting Bootsy off. "'Cause that's exactly what he got coming. All that other bullshit that he was spittin' in that letter, that shit might've touched Monica's heart, but it didn't convince me to let the matter go."

"Shit, me neither. The letter just let me know for real just how soft this coward ass nigga is. What type of gangsta out here in these streets would write a goddamn letter to a bitch who intended to take his ass out of this world? Man, had I survived an attempt like that and knew exactly where I could find that bitch, I would kill her and every fucking body around her!"

"You got that shit right. And that's what it is, and how it's got to be, my nigga," spat Ricky.

"I'm solid on that," responded Bootsy. "But looka here, man, 'cause I need for you to know this."

"What's that, dawg?" spat Ricky.

"I need for you to know that no matter what we go through, or what our opinions may be about this or that, I will never cross you, Ricky. I mean that shit, man. It's death before dishonor."

"That's what it is. And the love is mutual. Now peep this: While I was in jail, I met this cat who was in the same holding tank as me. The nigga was there for some type of domestic bullshit. I think he whipped his girl's ass or something. But me and the nigga were conversating and shit and he was telling me about some major moves he was making and shit down here."

"What type of moves, bruh?"

"Major kilos, Bootsy. The nigga large."

"Word, fam...?"

"That's on my solid. I told the nigga I had a spot and could move some shit. Guess what the nigga said? The nigga looked me in my eyes, Bootsy, and told me he would drop three of them thangz on me on consignment if I'm serious about getting money."

"What?" replied Bootsy.

"Fuck yeah."

"So what did you tell the nigga after he told you that?"

"I told the nigga I was for real about getting loot. So, he gave me a number and shit. I just haven't called."

"Shit, why not, dawg?"

"'Cause this Yolanda shit been on my mind heavy. Plus, I was seriously thinking about leaving this shit alone. But you know what?"

"What's that, dawg?"

"I might be facing some FED time for that damn gun and shit. That's what my lawyer indicated, anyway. So shit, I gotta stack up as much bread as I can. Feel me?"

"Definitely," replied Bootsy.

"So, that important shit I told you I had to take care of, contacting this dude about becoming our connection is what's up."

"We need to take care of that ASAP," Bootsy replied.

"We 'bout to do that right now," said Ricky, pulling up to a nearby phone booth to make the call.

*****

William was in the bedroom of Emily's crib, contemplating how many karats he wanted in the ring he had planned to put on Emily's finger when the phone started ringing.

He picked up after the third ring. "Hello," he answered.

"Yes, may I please speak to Emily?"

"She's not in at the moment. She's still at work. Can I take a message?"

"Just tell her, her cousin Rachael called."

"Rachael, what's up, girl?"

"Who is this?"

"Oh, what you don't know my damn voice now? This William."

"Damn, what's up, Will? I didn't even recognize your voice."

"Shit, I see that. What you doing in Savannah?"

"Not a damn thing. I do mean that literally. That was why I was calling Emily. She supposed to let me come stay with her."

"Really?"

"Yeah. She and I been talking about it lately. I just wanna experience something new.

Hell, I been here all my damn life. I'm tired of this place."

"I can dig it. It's ironic that you called though."

"You think so?" replied Rachael.

"Know so."

"Well, why you say that?"

"'Cause I was thinking about you last night, I ain't even gon' lie."

"You were thinking about me, huh? Tell me about that, 'cause to be honest I've had some thoughts of you as well since I left Charlotte."

"Well, I was just thinking about how your ass don't need to be smoking that high powdered ass weed that you and I had the last time I saw you." Rachael started laughing.

"No bullshit, Rachael. I'm serious."

"Why, Will?"

"Because you almost got my ass in some serious ass trouble with Emily."

"How?"

"Look, don't tell Emily I'm telling you this, but she heard your ass talking in your damn sleep about my damn dick."

"Hell no!"

"No, HELL YEAH! She wanted to kick my muthafuckin' ass, too. But I convinced her that you were just dreaming. And that I had not touched you at all."

"You told her that?"

"Shit, what you think I should have told her, the truth!?" Rachael laughed again. "No, I'm…I'm not saying that, Will."

"Whatchu saying then, Rachael?"

"Nothing. Hell, I can't say nothing. I'm really speechless. Honest, I am, but—"

William cut her off and said, "You know I came real close though, right?"

"You came real close?" she repeated, somewhat puzzled. "Close to what, Will?"

"Putting this dick on you."

"You did put it on me," replied Rachael.

"Nah, but I really wanted to. Emily came home in the nick of damn time."

"Not in my dream, she didn't."

"In your dream?"

"Yeah, in my dream. In my dream you fucked the hell out of me."

"Quit lying, Rachael."

"I swear to God. You lifted my lil skirt up and pulled my panties all the way off me. You rested my legs on your shoulders and fucked me with the biggest dick I have ever had inside my lil tight wet hole."

"You're serious, too, aren't you?" William questioned. The mere thought of this shit happening made his damn dick rock solid hard as he sat on Emily's bed.

"I'm dead ass serious, Will. You fucked me real good."

"What were you saying while my dick was planted up in you?"

"I was looking you in your eyes and saying if it's good to you, daddy, then hurt the muthafucka! You penetrated deep up in me when I said that."

"I did?" William asked, with his dick in his hand. He had taken it out of his pants and started stroking it with the Vaseline that was on top of Emily's nightstand. He couldn't control himself. Talking nasty had aroused him.

"Yeah, and after you put that big dick on me, you cleaned me up, because I had cum flowing from my cunt like a river. You then bent me over and asked me to position myself doggy-style. I thought you were about to fuck me in that position, but instead, you spread my pussy lips from the back and started licking my clit.

While you were doing that, you were fingering me. William, my whole body was trembling."

"Was it feeling that good, Rachael?" He lowered his voice in lust. His dick was long and hard as hell. He stroked it up and down as she talked.

"It was that good, Will. You did things with your tongue I didn't know a black guy could do. But then, while my ass was bent over, you stood up behind me and eased that big ass dick of yours back up in me. You didn't have any problem doing so because I was soaking fuckin' wet. The moment you put it back inside me, I started screaming at the top of my lungs. You were planted so deep within me, Will, I just couldn't take all of it from that position. So, you allowed me to reposition myself on my stomach with my ass tooted upward a little. Then you fucked me good and hard. In fact, the louder I screamed with my face buried in a pillow, the harder you thrust your dick in and out of me. Boy, you fucked me a long ass time, too. When I woke from that damn dream, the sheets on my bed were wet as hell from me having such a big ass orgasm!"

After Rachael said that there was sheer silence over the phone. William couldn't say shit. He was too busy beating his meat like he used to do when he was in prison, serving State time. When he was in prison serving State time, he used to beat his meat five and sometimes six times a day. That's all he did while serving his time was look at teen books and masturbate.

"Why in the hell did you get so quiet all of a sudden on me, Will?" You alright?"

"Ummm, hmmm. I'm straight." He then started inhaling hard through his teeth. "So you like how I was putting this dick on you, huh?" he asked in between stroking his dick up and down faster.

"Ummm, hmmm. I love that shit. And it would have been better in real life."

"Maybe one day you'll get your chance," he replied, feeling himself about to release.

"Fuckin' not if my cousin has anything to do with it."

"What she doesn't know won't hurt her at all, now will it?"

"It will, because after you fuck me, you ain't gonna want to fuck her anymore."

"You that damn good, huh?" he said, inhaling air through his teeth. He was nuttin' and shaking all at the same time.

"Damn right. This white country chick is just that good."

"You sure that ain't that good ass weed you had brought down here the last time you were here, talking? You know that shit be having you out of it."

"It ain't the weed talking. It's me. And everything about this good pussy'll make you turn in your lil playa card."

"Shit, your cousin 'bout to make me turn it in. You know I asked her to marry me, right?"

"I thought you were into selling coke and whatnot?"

"What that got to do with anything, Rachael?"

"Fuckin' 'lot. I don't know too many damn young drug dealers who are willing to forsake having a lot of chicks just to settle down with one."

"I love your cousin. She's been good to me over the years. Plus, I don't hustle anymore."

"That's a bunch of crap, Will! Stop it!"

"What's a bunch of crap?"

"The part about you don't hustle anymore."

"I don't, Rachael?"

"I just left y'all a week or so ago. And when I was there you showed me a helluva lot of cocaine."

"That shit gone, girl."

"So you're really through with it and ready to settle your ass down with my cousin, huh?"

"My only problem for real is keeping my damn dick in my pants. It's not hustling, Rachael."

"Umm, hmm. Well, that's just as bad. But look, I really shouldn't even be running this at you since you through hustling, but you know that killa weed I had when I was down there?"

"Yeah, that shit we smoked together, right?"

"Right. Well, Will, like I was sharing with you when I was down there, my father grows that shit. I got access to pounds upon pounds of it. I was thinking about putting you in on something."

"Like what, Rachael?"

"Like getting a lot of this shit in your hands so that we can make money down there in Charlotte. You do know people, right?"

"I know a lot of people. But shit, so does Emily."

"I don't want Emily really knowing about this. In fact, she don't even need to know that you and I are talking about something of this nature."

"Yeah, but Rachael, your cousin is gonna be my wife. She—"

"GONNA BE YOUR WIFE, William. Y'all haven't stood before the preacher yet. GONNA BE might not be until two or three years down the road. Now shit, you're a so- called PLAYA. Won't you play your cards right and let's find a way to get these pounds from Savannah to Charlotte."

William thought a moment. He had some grands stacked up from Emily, getting rid of all of his damn coke. He wanted to start him and Emily a small business doing something that he hadn't completely figured out yet. He knew it wouldn't be a problem getting rid of that weed. The shit was good stuff, just like the hustlers and niggas in the hood like it. *Maybe a few damn runs wouldn't hurt.*

He then said, "Rachael, give me a few days to think on it and I'll get back with you."

"How you gon' get back with me, Will, and you don't even have my number or nothing?"

"Emily got everything, doesn't she?"

"Will, looka here, you can't go asking Emily to give you my number and whatnot. My cousin too damn clever. She'll know something isn't right. So here, take down this number." Rachael gave William her hook up, "And make sure you call me within the next couple of days."

"I'ma do that. But Rachael check this out, I'm really surprised at you. I swear I am."

"Why, Will?"

"Because shit, you talk like you got hustler's sense."

"You crazy." She laughed. "Let's just say, I'M NO FOOL. Now, do what you gotta do so we can make some things happen. You wit' it?"

"I'ma holler at you in a few days. You'll know definitely if I'm with it or not then."

"Cool. In the meantime, keep that dick out of your hand. What, you think I didn't know that you were getting off while I was talking to you?"

"Bye, Rachael."

Rachael started laughing. "Bye, boy."

William disconnected their conversation, walked into Emily's bathroom and showered.

Freaky lil bitch, he said to himself, thinking of Rachael. *Freaky mutha'fuckin lil bitch..*

Chapter Twenty Two
[Something Is Being Hidden From Me.]

"Oh shit, Emily gurl, I forgot to tell you," said Shamika as her and Emily were in the parking lot of Southpark Mall. The both of them were getting off work. "My baby 'bout to come home."

"Who, girl?"

Shamika looked at Emily with her lips poked out and her hand on her hip. "Who else, Emily? Timothy, girl."

"Are you serious? I thought Timothy still had like a lot more time to do?"

"He did. But he called me yesterday evening and told me that due to the state system being overcrowded, they letting guys go home early who haven't been in any trouble and whatnot. Hell, my baby already done did like six years. He didn't have but fifteen."

"So they told him he's going home?" asked Emily.

"That's exactly what he told me. He called me and told me he'll be home Friday."

"Tomorrow?"

"Yep."

"William must not know about it, because his ass would have told me. That's his number one ace!"

"I swear he is, girl," agreed Shamika. You remember when the both of them were locked up and we used to take chances and shit, bringing them weed packed in balloons and shit?"

"Hell yeah, I remember. But shit, I had to do what I had to do for my man. And I'm glad I stuck by him, because girl, William been blessing the shit out of me. And guess what, Shamika, he asked me, down on his knees, to marry him."

"He did what?"

"You heard me girl. He wants me to be his wife."

"So did you say yes?"

"I did, but honestly, I think I said that shit too damn fast. I ain't really ready for marriage life right now. I'm too damn afraid, Shamika."

"Of what?"

"The fucking unknown."

"Y'all been together for a minute now, Emily. Whatchu mean you're afraid of the unknown? Shit, you know the nigga like the back of your hands."

"I don't know. I haven't been sleeping good lately. I've been some bad ass dreams, Shamika."

"Bad dreams about what, Emily? Talk to me."

"About him. William. I dreamed three times in the same night that I was looking out of this big ass window and I saw him running with a real terrified look on his face.

In all three dreams, Shamika, it was nighttime and I couldn't make out the face of the person chasing him. I just know he was running, trying to get away from whoever it was."

"You had this same dream three times you say, Emily?"

"Three damn times, girl."

"Did you tell him?"

"No. But I plan to."

"That's some strange shit. Might even be some type of warning. Tell me, have you been noticing anything unusual about him? You know people tend to not be able to hide everything, Emily. And if you pay close attention you'll pick up on what it is you need to pick up on."

Emily inhaled and exhaled hard. She then looked down at the concrete of the parking lot and reflected.

"I ain't gon' lie, 'cause you my friend Shamika. But you know William just got out of prison not long ago, right?"

"Like six, or seven months ago, right?" replied Shamika.

"Something like that. Well, he called me not many days ago and asked me to come pick him up because it was an emergency. My cousin Rachael was down here from Savannah at that time so I took her along with me to go get his ass. The first thing I noticed though when I picked him up was that he had blood all over his all white Timberland Hoody. He claimed that he was in a fight. I knew he was a thug and thugs always getting into something. So shit, I didn't pay a lot of attention to that. But something else caught my attention later on."

"What was that?" asked Shamika. "And hurry up, Emily, cause you know how that five and six o'clock traffic is."

"He had this pillowcase in his hand that I later found out was full as hell of coke and cash. And I'm not talking about a little bit of shit, Shamika."

"Damn, he must have come up on a serious ass connection. Probably met a goddamn Columbian, or one of them damn Mexicans."

Emily looked at Shamika with serious doubt in her eyes. "I don't think so, because I helped him get rid of the shit, and I noticed he didn't say shit about having to pay anybody anything."

"So then, how do you think he got it?"

"That's what been puzzling me. But that's not all, Shamika. On the night that he proposed to me, down on his knees and shit, he had a big ass gash at the side of his neck. He told me he almost lost his life. But he never went into details on that.

I just feel something is being hidden from me."

"If it is, Emily, it'll come out. Trust that. 'Cause, what's done in the dark eventually comes to the light. Now, call me later on or betta yet, I'll call you."

"Okay, Shamika." The both of them then got into their rides and headed home.

Chapter Twenty Three
[Bitterness Is a Dangerous Emotion]

"You told Harpo to beat me," Oprah Winfrey said to Whoopi Goldberg in Monica's favorite movie, *The Color Purple*. She and little Ali were lying in her bed watching it. The both of them had dozed off, but Monica awoke when she heard a voice calling her name. She looked over at the clock on her nightstand. It read fifteen after midnight. She picked Ali up and carried him in his room and tucked him into his bed, being ever so careful not to awaken him. She then walked back to her bedroom, turned her television off and prepared herself to call it a night. But calling it a night wouldn't come easy.

As she lay on her bed on her back looking upward at the ceiling, she heard a voice calling her name again, "Monica." The voice was coming from the stairway. Monica, got up and retrieved her 38 revolver from underneath her mattress. She walked out of her bedroom to the top of the stairway with her gun in hand.

"Monica, O' Monica," the voice said again. It was a feminine voice. One in which Monica was all too familiar with. This time though, she recognized that the voice was coming from the direction of her bedroom. She turned her body toward her bedroom and pointed her 38 straight forward. What she saw made her rub her hand over her eyes. The right eye first, then the left one for clear vision. She was beholding Yolanda. And Yolanda was standing there at her bedroom doorway. She was braless just like she was prior to Monica killing her in real life. "You can put your gun away, Monica. You can't do to me a second time what you did unto me the first. Guns made by man could never kill a spirit made by God."

Monica again rubbed her hand over both her eyes. She couldn't believe that she was actually having a vision. "Why are you here?" she asked, trembling.

"Why shouldn't I be here, Monica? You're my sister and I love you."

Death, No Exceptions!

"Just leave and don't come back."

"Love won't allow me to do that, Monica."

"You don't love me. How could you love me and put my business out in the streets as you did?"

"I told you before you ended my life on earth that I made an honest mistake."

"That's a lame excuse and you know it! You knew the game. You knew that loose lips sink ships! Ricky and Bootsy always told you and I that. So Yolanda you knew better."

"I didn't come to argue, Monica."

"Then dammit, leave! 'Cause all I have for you is an argument. You ruined my life and caused my son to go through life absent a finger. All because you couldn't zip your damn lips!"

"I was under the influence of alcohol."

"It doesn't matter, dammit! Just like you shouldn't fucking drink and drive. You shouldn't damn drink and run your fucking mouth! Especially when you know something might come out of it that might jeopardize someone else's security."

"If the world was perfect, Monica, not a one of us would have any gripes. Again, I say, I made an honest mistake."

"It's not about the world being PERFECT! It's about a nigga being on POINT out here! One slip or wrong turn could lead to death, no exceptions. Or did you forget!?"

"I forgot nothing. And again, I didn't come to argue. I came to let you know that I forgive you."

"You forgive me, huh? Well, don't forgive me. Forgive yourself!!"

"Bitterness is a dangerous emotion, Monica. So is vengeance when it is not balanced with mercy."

"Listen, dammit! Don't confuse me with being bitter. I was bruised. There's a difference!"

"Bruises heal, in time," Yolanda said softly.

When Yolanda said that, she vanished. Monica was left standing in her hallway facing her bedroom doorway with her gun in hand. She still had it pointing forward. She put it down at the side of her legs when she heard little Ali say, "Momma, who were you screaming at?" She hurried and put her gun in the pocket of her bed robe. She turned towards Ali.

She walked over to him and got down on her knees. She hugged him tight. "Mommie wasn't screaming at nobody, baby," she lied, looking him into his eyes.

"But I heard you, Momma. You was talking to somebody like you wuz mad."

"Mommie was just talking to herself, baby. That's all you heard. Go on back to bed."

When Monica said that, she looked into little Ali's room and saw Yolanda sitting on his bed. This time Yolanda was dressed in all white. She held in her arms a small teddy bear that Ali sleeps with every night. "Why don't you tell him the truth, Monica? Why don't you tell him that you shot and killed the woman who was a true sister to you, and a true aunt to him? Tell your son what being motivated by a spirit of uncompromising revenge leds you to do."

Monica didn't want Ali to hear her again talking to someone he couldn't see. She noticed also that Yolanda had vanished again. "C'mon, Ali. You can sleep in here with Mommie tonight, okay?"

"Yes, ma'am," he replied, nodding his head up and down. Monica picked him up and carried him into her room. That's when she heard her phone ring. Monica tucked Ali in her bed then answered her phone. "What up?" she asked, after about three rings.

"Monica, what's up, baby? This Bootsy."

"What's up, Bootsy? Where you at?"

"Hanging over here at Snaggle Cat's, fucking with Ricky."

"How are y'all doing over that way?"

"Shit, slow at the moment. We 'bout to make some moves though. What took you so long to answer your phone?"

"I was tucking Ali in bed."

"Damn. This fucking late, Monica?"

"This fucking late, yes, Bootsy. Now, what else you wanna know?"

"Can I come over? That's what I really call to ask; can I come over?"

"Can you come over?" she repeated him.

"Yeah. Like I said, shit slow as hell over here."

"So that's why you wanna come over 'cause things SLOW over there. Huh, Bootsy?"

"Nah, Monica, I don't mean it like that. I just—"

"Boy, I been around you and damn Ricky long enough to know that with y'all it's dollars over dating," she spat cutting him off. "Besides. it's late."

"Monica, check this shit out. You ain't no date to me. You are my damn darling. Why you—?"

"I'm your darling? Nigga, Bootsy, you ought to stop it," she said, cutting him off.

"Whatchu think? I'm blowing smoke up your ass, or something, Monica?"

"You might be," she spat, while cuddling with Ali.

"I love you too fuckin' much to do that. And for the record, even if it wasn't slow over here, I would still rather be next to you any day."

"Ummm hmmm, I hear you talkin'," Monica said, sucking her teeth.

"Can I come over or not? If you don't want me to I'll understand."

"Look, Bootsy. It's well after twelve and I'm in the bed with my son."

"Our son."

"Now you his daddy, huh? Boy you somethin', you know that?"

"I love little Ali just like I love you."

"Nigga kill that love shit. It's late; I'm in my damn panties and bra. And, in the goddamn bed with my son."

"Our son."

"Don't cut me off again, Bootsy. Now call me tomorrow, you and Ricky."

"A'ight then, whatever, Monica."

"Ya lil ass mad as fuck now, huh? Whatever, Bootsy."

"You right, whatever."

Bootsy disconnected their conversation and sat in place for a moment. He really wanted Monica as his woman. Nothing meant more to him at this moment in his life than having her. He blew air hard from his mouth, causing his jaws to inflate. *Fuck it!* He then got up and went looking for Ricky.

He found Ricky in Snaggle Cat's den. He and Snaggle Cat were having what appeared to be a deep conversation. Bootsy elected not to interrupt. Besides, he had other things on his mind. He went back into the kitchen, picked up the phone and started dialing Monica's number. He heard the phone ring once, before he said to himself, *Fuck it*, and hung up. He shot back into the den where Ricky and Snaggle Cat were talking. "Rick, I'ma bounce a minute. I'll be back."

"A'ight, dawg. I'll be here."

"I got your car, too, a'ight?"

"Go ahead, bruh. I ain't sweatin' that shit. Like I said, I'll be here."

Bootsy took the car and bounced. He got to Monica's crib in no time. Less than twenty minutes, to be exact. He phoned her from Ricky's car phone while in her driveway. She answered on the second ring. "Hello."

"Monica, get out of bed and let me in, I'm in your driveway."

"Boy, why are you so damn hardheaded? Didn't I tell you it was late?"

"Get up and open the door, a'ight? I'm getting out of the car now."

"Boot—" Before Monica could say anything further, she heard the dial tone from him hanging up. She got up out of bed like her ass was in a race. She was gonna curse Bootsy out for hanging up on her if nothing else.

"Nigga, don't you ever hang the phone up on me while I'm still fucking talking. You hear me?" Monica barked the moment she let Bootsy inside her condo. She was pointing her finger in his face at his nose.

"Whatever. Put some damn clothes on," Bootsy shot back, sidestepping her and moving her finger out of his face.

"I don't have to put on shit if I don't want to. I pay the bills here." Monica was in such a hurry to check him for hanging up the phone, that she abandoned placing her bed robe on. Instead, she stood before Bootsy in here panties and bra.

"Why you got to be hollering, Monica? You gon' wake Ali up and shit with all that."

Monica lowered her voice a little, got up in Bootsy's face and said, "So fucking what if I do!? Don't you be hanging up the damn phone while I'm talking to you? Now, you ever do that shit again, me and you gon' have some problems."

"Yes ma'am, Miss Bad Ass! Whatchu got in this kitchen to eat? I'm hungry."

"Not a damn thing. You should've ate before you came."

"Stop lying, Monica," Bootsy said, walking into her kitchen. She followed right behind him. She saw him look into her refrigerator. "You got all types of shit up in here."

He took out a box of leftover Domino's pizza and put a couple of slices in the microwave. Monica just stood at the entrance of her kitchen door looking on.

"I thought I told you it was late and that I was in the bed with my son, boy?"

"You did, but shit, I wanted to see you and talk."

"Bootsy, there's a time and place for everything. You just don't show up over here wanting to see and talk to me absent my permission. What if I had a guy friend over here or something?"

"If you did, you would have told me. And for the record, if you would have told me that you had a guy friend over here; his ass would have had to leave. No jokin', because I better be the only man coming over here. Unless it's Ricky."

"You are not my man, Bootsy. You ain't running nothing here."

"I tell you what! Have a man other than my brother Ricky over here, around my son Ali, and see what happens to him."

"When Bootsy made that statement, the buzzer went off on the microwave.

"I think I said it clear enough. You are not my man," she said, walking out of the kitchen and into her living room. She then returned seconds later and saw Bootsy standing facing the microwave and placing two slices of pizza on a plate. When he turned around to walk and then sit at the table, he saw Monica standing there with her hand on her hip, leaning on the side of her refrigerator. He noticed that she had put on a Chicago Bulls' starters sweater to cover her breast. Bootsy slightly laughed and said, "If you're gonna cover yourself up, don't half-step. Go all the way." He saw that although her breasts were now covered, she still had on her panties and tube socks.

"If I wanna walk around in MY house NAKED, I can. It's my prerogative. Told you, I pay the bills up in here. Now, answer my question. Whatchu doing showing up over here this late without me signing off on it?"

"First of all, why you gotta be standing way over there talking to me? Can't you at least have a seat next to me at this table?"

"No! Now, answer my question."

"Told you, I want to see you and talk," he said, chewing his food.

"You saw me earlier today. You didn't have much to talk about then. Won't you just keep it real, Bootsy, and just say that because y'all lil dope spot ain't pumping hard tonight, that you got fucking bored and decided that out of your boredom you would try to set up you a booty call with Monica. Well, you betta believe I'm not that easy!"

Bootsy stopped chewing his pizza and looked at Monica strange. "Booty Call? You're not that easy?!" he repeated. "You actually think I would disrespect you like that, Monica?"

Monica didn't respond. She just stood there before him with her lips poked outward, her arms folded over her breast area and moving her leg side-to-side as if nervous.

"If you think that shit then Monica I'm 'bout to eat this pizza and bounce the fuck up outta here. Matta fact, fuck it! I'm bouncin'."

Bootsy didn't even give himself a chance to eat the pizza he had remaining on his plate. Instead, he wiped his mouth with a napkin and got up to walk past Monica into the living room and out her front door. Monica had really offended him with her view of why he was over at her place at such a late hour.

She sensed this reality from Bootsy's now upset demeanor and grabbed his lower arm where his wrist was as he was proceeding to bypass her on his way out.

"Wait. Wait, Bootsy! I didn't mean it like that. Don't leave, finish eating your pizza."

"How the hell else could you have not meant it, Monica? Huh? You don't usually say shit you don't mean."

"I didn't mean it. Now sit down and finish eating."

Bootsy shook his head in the negative, "Nah, I'm straight, I'm outta here. Now let go of my arm."

"I ain't letting go of shit. Now finish eating like I said."

"How the fuck can I when your little mis-fucking-understanding of me has caused me to lose my damn appetite?"

"Lower your voice before my son hears you."

"Look, Monica, whatever. Just let my muthafuckin' arm go so I can bounce. 'Cause shit, if you think that all a nigga want from you is some muthafuckin' pussy, you got me twisted!"

Monica didn't say anything. She just held his arm with a tight grip and looked deep into his eyes with her lips poked out.

"You can look at me like that all you want to, Monica. But you wrong. I could've called any lil bitch out there that I be hollering at and shit on the low when a nigga wanna fuck! But I don't want any of them lil street chicks. A nigga wanted to just come over here and sit and talk to you. It ain't have shit to do with just being bored!"

"All I'm saying is that it's late, Bootsy, and I was in bed."

"That's not all you were fuckin' saying, Monica! You fuckin' indicated that my call, to my muthafuckin' cutie, was a BOOTY CALL. And you're wrong."

"Okay, Bootsy, I was wrong. I'm sorry."

"Apology accepted. Now let me go."

"So you leaving?" Monica asked, letting his arm go and looking him in his eyes.

"Yeah, I'm leaving. I'm upset. And there's no need for me to stick around and try talking to you when I'm in my feelings."

"But I said, I apologize."

"And I said, apology accepted. But I don't need to be here right now."

"So where you're going then? To be with one of your girls?"

"What's it to you? I'm not your man, remember?"

When Bootsy said that, he walked away and left Monica standing in the kitchen. He exited her condo. He wanted to slam the hell out of the door on his way out, he was so upset. But since little Ali was upstairs asleep, he put the brakes on that thought and just left quietly.

Monica walked into her living room when she heard her door shut. She looked from the window in her living room and saw Bootsy exiting her driveway. She inhaled and exhaled hard, then turned to go upstairs into her bedroom. Midway up the stairs, she looked up and saw Yolanda again.

"Girl, you just don't know how much you offended Bootsy with your remark. That boy been trying to holler at you, and he's been very patient in his pursuit. But what you do? You run him off with words from your mouth that should have never come out. The last thing Bootsy wants is what's between your legs, Monica. He wants you. But guess what? You're too blind and bitter to see that. And you had the nerve to not forgive me for something that I should not have said while I was on earth. At least I was under the influence of alcohol. What's your excuse?"

"Whatever my excuse is," Monica hissed, "it's my goddamn business!"

"You're right. You are absolutely right. But trust this, that's the type of business and attitude that never pays off well."

"What-fuckin'-ever! Just get the fuck up out."

Before Monica could complete her sentence, Yolanda had vanished. Monica placed her hand over the bridge of her nose and took in a deep breath before exhaling and making her way back to her bedroom. There while sitting on the very edge of her bed, she thought how she had offended Bootsy. It really made her feel bad that she had done so, because not only had he been a comfort to her, post Yolanda's death. But she could talk to him about anything. *Why did I not just shut my damn mouth and listen to whatever it was he wanted to share with me? And why the fuck won't Yolanda stay her ass in her grave and stop appearing to me? Don't the bitch know that she's dead? Damn!* Monica then got up from her bed, grabbed herself two sleeping tablets from her medicine cabinet in her bathroom and down them, in hopes of them putting her straight to sleep so that she wouldn't have to toss and turn with thoughts of having hurt Bootsy and her mind playing tricks on her with visions of Yolanda.

Chapter Twenty Four
[Why Do You Love Me]

After exiting Monica's crib and riding around in the city for a while to reflect and cool off, Bootsy arrived back at Snaggle Cat's place. As he sat momentarily in the driveway, he looked at the time on the clock of Ricky's dashboard. It read 2:20 a.m. He shook away thoughts of Monica offending him and elected to think on the moves he and Ricky were about to make. Major moves. The guy Ricky had met while briefly locked up, whom Ricky phoned earlier had informed Ricky that if he could meet him at a certain location tomorrow, Ricky would be glad that he did. Ricky and Bootsy took that to mean that it was on! Thinking on it while sitting in the car had Bootsy's adrenaline flowing, because if this guy was gonna indeed bless Ricky with a large quantity of coke, it could mean big things poppin'.

*****

"Ricky, next week I'll be checkin' into rehab. I told you, I'm about to be through with this addiction. I'm serious."

"Shit, I'm all for you, Snaggle Cat. I want you to be through with it so that you can start getting some real muthafuckin' money, 'cause shit 'bout to get serious."

"In what way, Ricky? 'Cause you sound like you got something up your sleeve."

"I do," he replied. He then sat next to her real close. She was at her kitchen table, helping him bag cocaine. "Look, Snag, I'm about to get my damn hands on a lot of shit."

"A lot of shit like what? I know you're not talking about cocaine, Ricky?"

"Damn right, that's what I'm talking about. Now—"

"You said you was considering leaving this shit alone. Now you got a lot of money, Ricky. Why don't you just let this shit go? There ain't no real future in this shit."

"I know all that. But fuck it, I might be going to jail. The more paper I stack now, the less I'll have to worry about doin' it once I return home."

"But, Ricky, you don't know for sure yet that you're gonna have to do time. Hell, you might beat the shit."

"I might. Then again, I might not. I just gotta hope for the best but prepare for the worse."

"Well, look," Ricky said, cutting her off. "While you're there, Bootsy and I are still gonna be holding this spot down. Don't worry about it getting too hot over here. We gon' take care all of that. You know how he and I do it anyway. People come, get their shit, and they keep it moving."

Snaggle Cat stopped what she was doing a moment and placed her hand over Ricky's.

"Ricky, let me ask you something that I have always wanted to ask you."

"What's that, Snag?"

"I know I get high and whatnot. But do you really love me? Tell me the truth."

Ricky looked Snaggle Cat in her eyes. Even though her question caught him off guard, answering it was a no brainer. "Of course I love you. Shit, you're like a big sister. You getting high don't have anything to do with that. Fuck, we all do something we really shouldn't be doing."

"Yeah, but Ricky why?"

"Why what? Snaggle Cat."

"Why do you love me like you do? I mean, you even trusted me with going into your stash. Ricky, I can't get over that."

When she said that, both of them saw Bootsy walk in. He came and sat directly at the table with them and started helping to bag coke. "Damn, dawg, you look like something on your mind and shit. You a'ight?" asked Ricky.

"Oh foe 'sho' my nigga, I'm straight. Just Monica, dawg. She trippin' and shit."

"Well, you know how she is," Ricky responded.

Bootsy shrugged his shoulders. "Oh, I know. What's up with y'all though?"

"Ain't shit, Bootsy," said Snaggle Cat.

"Bootsy, Snag wants to know why I love her so much," interjected Ricky.

"You mean, why we love her so much," Bootsy said, looking over at Snaggle Cat. She was blushing hard as hell. "Shit, how could we not love her when she has always kept it real?

"Remember when Bootsy and I first met you? He and I remember it good because we talk about it often," said Ricky.

 "Yeah, I remember. I was carrying my groceries out of A&P grocery store when the two of you were getting into your Cadillac. Some fuckin' maniac snatched my damn purse right off of my arm and hauled ass. I had just gotten my damn check cashed, too."

Ricky slightly laughed and said, "It's funny because Bootsy the one who heard you scream. He was like, "Yo' Ricky, that nigga just snatched that woman's purse!"Before I knew it, Bootsy was hauling ass after him. I didn't even know that my lil brother here could run that damn fast. But he caught up to that nigga and beat that muthafucka with his 9mm till the nigga's face was so covered with blood, that had I not gotten Bootsy up off the nigga, he probably would have killed him!"

Bootsy shook his head and cracked a smile, while Ricky continued. "When I went to get Bootsy up off that nigga, all I could hear Bootsy saying while beating the fuck out of him was, NIGGA, DON'T YOU EVER IN YO' LIFE SNATCH A PURSE FROM A MU-THA-FUC-KIN' WORKING WOMAN!" Snaggle Cat looked over at Bootsy and rubbed her hand over his arm in remembrance of what he did as Ricky brought the matter back to her attention.

"After getting my purse back, y'all told me I didn't have to wait on a taxi, because y'all would give me a ride home. That's exactly what y'all did too. Drove me straight here," said Snaggle Cat.

"Yeah, but neither Ricky nor me was prepared for what you asked after we drove you here," said Bootsy.

"I know, I know, I know," Snaggle Cat replied, smiling.

"You looked over at Ricky when we carried your bags into your house and said, "If neither of you don't mind me asking, do y'all know where I can get me a couple pieces of crack?"

"Yeah, but you know why I asked y'all that though, right?" asked Snaggle Cat. "I asked y'all that because I could tell y'all were drug boys. Y'all had on nice ass clothes, jewelry and all that. And guess what? I was right like a muthafucka. 'Cause Ricky pulled out a big ass bag of coke and served me well that day. I'll never forget it."

"Well, we can go on and on with that story. That was really just the beginning. What really locked you in with me and Bootsy for real was that time we were up in the kitchen right here and unbeknownst to us; the cops were at your door. Bootsy and I had muthafuckin' cocaine every damn where. We were in here and heard the cops asking you can they come inside, because they had gotten a call that drug activity was being conducted. We heard you say, "Well, what y'all heard is wrong, Mr. Police. And if y'all are gonna come up in here, y'all will need a search warrant. I'm sorry, those cops didn't come in either. It was at that moment that Bootsy and I fell in love with you, Snaggle Cat, 'cause if those cops would have come in, all three of us—me, you, and him—would have had to do some damn time in prison."

"You got that right," said Snaggle Cat. Bootsy also nodded his head in agreement.

"Shit, you our girl, Snaggle Cat. We gon' always love you. And that's a fact," spat Bootsy, with Ricky nodding in agreement.

"Oh, but Ricky," Snaggle Cat said, hitting Ricky on the arm, "What about that time you had me over here. I think you came to pick up some clothes that I had gotten out of the cleaners for you. And some girl was in your car. A nice looking dark-skinned girl, too. She saw me hug you and kiss you on your cheek right outside of your car. I remember she got out of your car and said, "Ricky, I know you ain't disrespecting me by allowing another bitch to be affectionate with you like that! Whoever that chick was, I swear if you wouldn't have held me back with them strong ass hands of yours and said something to her, she and I would have rumbled that day."

Ricky looked over at Bootsy and laughed, "You know who Snaggle Cat talking about, right?"

"Who, Monica?" replied Bootsy.

"Nah. She talking about Yolanda."

Death, No Exceptions!

"Yeah, that's the name I heard you address her by. Yolanda. That girl screamed on you about me giving you that hug and kiss, Ricky. I'll never forget that. Who was she anyway, Ricky? Was she your girlfriend?" asked Snaggle Cat.

Ricky put his elbows on top of the table. He put his hands together and rested his chin on top of them and looked off for a moment as if having to think before answering Snaggle Cat's question. After a few seconds of being in this posture, he inhaled and exhaled hard, got up from the table, rubbed his hand over and across Snaggle Cat's shoulder and said, "That girl was my sweetheart. She's dead now, Snaggle Cat. Dead and gone."

Snaggle Cat placed her hand on top of the hand that Ricky rubbed her shoulder with. She then looked up at him and said, "I'm sorry to hear that, Ricky. I really am."

"I'll be outside. I need some fresh air," Ricky said. Snaggle Cat looked over at Bootsy, who shrugged his shoulders and said, "He's strong. He'll be all right. I know him. He'll be just fine. Now let's get back to baggin' this coke."

Chapter Twenty Five
[I'm In A Better Place]

Ricky walked out of Snaggle Cat's crib into her front yard. The wind was blowing not too cool, not too hot. It was just a nice ass breeze for 3:00 something in the morning.

Ricky stood out in the yard with his hands propped on his waist looking outward.

"Ricky," an audible voice spoke. He turned aside and saw that it was Yolanda. Her hair was longer than it was prior to her death, and it was blowing in the wind. Ricky noticed that she was wearing a very beautiful pink gown, which was also blowing in the wind. Her feet never touched the ground.

"Yo-lan-da?" he said, stretching his eyes.

"It's me, Ricky. Let it go, ba-by. The whole thing about me getting killed, let it go."

"I can't, Yolanda. I just can't. It hurts too bad for me to do that."

"Never say what you can't do, Ricky. If you go and kill somebody just to soften the blow of my death on your heart, it won't bring me back, Ricky. It won't. So what's the use?

"The guy who is behind all of this is still walking the earth somewhere. I got to confront him, Yolanda. I have to. It's the only way I'm ever gonna feel some type of closure for what ultimately happened to you. There's no way I can just let it go like that."

"I'm at peace now, Ricky. That's all over here, peace. There's no way I can be exposed to what I am exposed to now and promote war. Please, just let it go. In time the hurt will heal."

"That I can't do, Yolanda," Ricky replied, shaking his head in the negative.

"Look, Ricky, I know my death hurt you. It hurt you because you love me. I didn't really know how much you loved me, but now I know. And—"

"How could you know now, Yolanda? I don't understand you saying that," he said, cutting her off.

"It's not easy to explain. But let's just say I have been watching over you ever since my demise. I saw you crying in secret, and I saw how you reacted to Monica for not having mercy on me. I'm with you everyday, Ricky. Everyday. And I understand, baby, trust me."

"I really, really love you, Yolanda. And I miss you like crazy," Ricky said. Tears started falling down his eyes and face.

"I know you do, Ricky. But like I said, I'm in a better place. Furthermore, baby, let me share something with you about love. Real love frees an individual who has been hurt or harmed by another, from all acts of vengeance. Now that's hard for a lot of human beings to accept, because on earth, fighting fire with fire is the norm, especially when you're thuggin' in the streets. But with God, Ricky, ALL THINGS ARE POSSIBLE. In addition, real love allows one to be content in knowing that no life, be it great, or small, can depart from the earth, absent God's permission. Take it, or leave it, Ricky, but God alone is the giver and taker of life."

When Yolanda said that, Ricky turned around and saw Bootsy approaching. Bootsy walked up to Ricky and clearly saw Ricky's tear-stained cheek. He knew from seeing such, that Ricky was having one of his moments. "I just came out here to check on you, bruh. Is everything alright?" Bootsy asked, looking Ricky in the eyes.

Ricky unashamedly wiped his face with the sleeve of his Khaki polo shirt. He then took a deep breath and exhaled slowly. "All is well, lil bruh.

All is well."

Chapter Twenty Six
[Put My Nigga on the Phone]

[Ring...Ring...Ring...] "Hello," answered Emily with her eyes barely open.

"Yeah, who dis? Emily?"

"Yeah, what's up?" she said with a low voice.

"This Timothy."

"Damn, it's early as hell, Timothy. What's up though, boy?"

"Ain't shit. Guess what though?"

"What?"

"I'll be out of this bitch today. I'm coming home, girl!"

"Shit, I'm glad you are. You know Shamika need yo' ass."

"I know, right? Where my nigga at though?"

"His ass right here. Wanna speak to him?"

"Hell naw. I wanna talk to yo' ass all morning," Timothy said, laughing.

"You still crazy, boy."

"Put my nigga on the phone."

"Will. Will. Getcha ass up. Timothy on the phone," Timothy heard Emily say as she was proceeding to pass William the phone.

"Hello," William said.

"Nigga, get yo' ass up out that bed, 'cause yo' nigga will be home in a few hours and you know what it is!"

"Quit lying, nigga. You still got time to do."

"Not anymore. Due to over crowdedness, I'm on my way out this bitch. Like today, my nigga."

"Who coming to getcha?"

"Shit, Shamika wants to, but man, if her ass come get me, she and I gon' be fuckin' like a muthafucka!"

"What's wrong with that? You do want you some pussy, don't you?"

"Goddamn right! But I want my ass some money, too. So for real, for real, I called to see if you could come get me. Think you can?"

"Man, I got a hot ass candy apple red, chromed out 300ZX. I bought that bitch cheap, but she ain't hardly got no miles on her at all. So whatchu mean, do I think I can come get you? My nigga, I'ma be there. What time you gon' be walking out them doors?"

"An hour before noon."

"What, eleven o'clock?"

"Yeah."

"You still at Morganton High Rise?"

"Yep."

"I'll be there in no time. Matta fact, I gotta get my ass up anyway, 'cause

I gotta stop by my Auntie Pearl's place. You remember me talking about her when we were locked up together, right?"

"You know I do. Just be here on time, Will. A nigga can't wait to hit them damn streets."

"I gotchu, my nigga."

"A'ight then, I'll see you when I see you."

"Fo' sho'."

William hung up the phone. He then started rubbing on and over Emily's ass cheeks. She was laying sideways with her ass tooted all up on his dick. He was hard as hell as a result. Plus, she didn't have on any panties, just one of his T-shirts. "Can I get a lil bit, baby?" William whispered in her ear as his finger rubbed over her clit.

"It's too damn early, Will, and I'm damn tired. Hell, we been fuckin' all damn night."

"And?" William shot back. "What that got to do with me getting a lil piece this morning before I bounce, baby?"

"Because my damn pussy sore, boy."

"I'll be gentle, baby," William assured, while at the same time rubbing his finger in circular motion on her clit. She was getting wet as water in spite of her pussy being sore from them fucking all night.

"You always holler you gon' be gentle. But when yo' ass get started, you end up beating my damn pussy up," Emily said. "Now stop and let me rest." She removed his finger from her clit although it was feeling so damn good. But William wasn't going out like that.

So he said, "Well, baby, since ya' pussy sore, give me some ass." William knew Emily loved it when he fucked her up her ass. He grabbed the KY jelly from the drawer of the nightstand and saturated his dick with it. He then, while she was still laying sideways to him with her ass tooted downward, lifted one of her legs and placed his dick in her asshole. "You gon' fuck regardless, aren't you?" Emily lifted her shirt to play with her titty while he fuck her. William eased his KY jelly saturated dick in her asshole, inch by inch, and started pumping in an out gently. "You like that, baby?" he whispered in her ear. She inhaled air through her teeth. "Ummm hmmm. Finger my clit while your dick is in my ass, Will." She moaned, getting into it. William started fingering the hell out of her clit while his hard thick dick was buried deep up her ass. She used one of her hands to caress her titty. And her eyes nearly rolled upward in the back of her head as he pumped his dick in and out of her and flicked his finger up and down her clit. William felt her body shaking, "Oh, gosh, Will, I'm com-com, O' Lord, I'm coming."

"Me, too, baby." William moaned as he pumped in and out of her harder. William exploded inside her anal canal. She knew his ass was releasing himself all in her, because his pace decreased. "I love you, girl," he said, taking himself out of her. He noticed her body was still shaking. He tongue kissed her hard, then smacked her on her ass cheek and went to shower.

After William showered, he put on a tan and dark brown shirt and short outfit, with his matching tan and dark brown quarter cut Filas. He kissed Emily on her forehead before he decided to bounce. Her ass was knocked out from that good dick he placed on her. Thirty minutes later, he was pulling into his Auntie Annie Pearl's driveway. He turned down his music, which was blasting through his Kenwood high-amped speakers. The bass in his speakers sent shockwaves all through Annie Pearl's neighborhood. Before he turned his music down, he was pumpin' "Fuck the Police," by his favorite ole school rap group, NWA. He exited his chromed-out candy apple red Nissan 300ZX. The time on his watch read eight o'clock on the dot.

William knew she had to be in her kitchen, cooking breakfast, because he could smell the aroma of bacon frying. He didn't eat pork, but he sure as hell loved the way it smelled.

"Who's there?" Annie Pearl asked. "Is that you, William?"

"Yes, ma'am, Annie Pearl, it's me."

"Figured so when I heard that loud music. I don't know why y'all young people play y'all music so loud in ya cars and stuff," she said standing with her dishrag in her hand, her white apron on, and her hand on her hip as he walked up and over to her and gave her a kiss on the cheek. "How's my ole girl doin'?"

"I'm fine. You hungry?"

"Not really. Just fix me an egg sandwich, 'cause I'm really in a hurry."

"You always in a hurry."

"Well, I want to stay longer, Auntie Pearl, but I gotta take a trip out of town to pick up a friend of mine who is coming home today."

"Mmmm hmmm. Well, have a seat a moment, 'cause I got something for you. I was hoping to give it to you sooner, but you don't come over here but ever so often."

"I know, and I'm sorry, Auntie Pearl."

"You don't have to be sorry. Just be a little more thoughtful. Now stay put, I'll be right back."

After about five good minutes, Annie Pearl returned with her pocketbook in her hand. She saw William washing the egg sandwich that he had eaten down with a glass of cold milk. He then wiped his mouth with a napkin. Annie Pearl sat her pocketbook on the counter next to the sink.

She retrieved from it the envelop that William had given her with the ten thousand dollars inside it. She handed it to him.

"What's wrong, Auntie Pearl?" he asked, looking at her puzzled.

"You know exactly what's wrong. How could you give me dirty money, William? More less, bring it into my house?"

"Auntie Pearl, with all due respect, money is money."

"Not in this house, and you know that! Now what did you do to get that kind of money, William? Are you sellin' them drugs?"

William got silent, dropped his head and exhaled hard, causing his jaws to inflate.

"Auntie Pearl, do you really want me to answer that? 'Cause you know I'm not gonna lie to you?"

"I want you to get yourself together, before you end up back in prison or worse, dead in them streets!"

"Auntie Pearl, I just wanted to give you this money as a symbol of my appreciation for being the only mother I have ever known. That's—"

"I don't take drug money. Never have, William, and I never will. You wanna do something special for me, come see me more often and call me on a regular basis. It don't cost anything to do that, but your time. My days on this Earth now are short. You should wanna spend as much time with me as you can."

"I do," William replied.

"Then why don't you?!"

William couldn't answer that question. He could, but his response would not be a justifiable one. How could he tell the woman who had raised him from an infant because his own parents didn't want him, that the reason he couldn't spend quality time with her was because he had been too busy thuggin' in the streets, and putting his dick up in this girl and that girl. And how could he tell her that the scar on the side of his neck that she hadn't taken notice of, had come from a bullet that was inches from putting his ass in the dirt, six-feet deep, as a result of his own carelessness? Carelessness that has also caused him to keep a low profile in the city.

He thought on this a minute, then said, "God-willing, Auntie Pearl, I'm gonna start spending more time with you."

"God is always willing. The question is, are you? If you are, then you will put forth the effort. You wouldn't allow nothing, or no one to stop you from coming over here and spending time with your auntie on a regular basis. And don't make no excuse for yourself, 'cause grown mature folk don't make excuses."

"You're right, Auntie Pearl. I can't dispute what you're saying at all."

William then looked at his watch. It was eight-thirty. He knew he had to get going if he was gonna be in Morganton to pick Timothy up on time. He, therefore, cuffed the money that his auntie had given him back, underneath his left armpit.

"I'ma call you later this evening when I come back from out of town, Auntie Pearl. I gotta be on my way right now, or I'ma be late." He kissed her and hugged her with one arm.

"All I can say, William, is try to stay out of trouble. God knows the devil is busy out there."

"Yes, ma'am. I'll try."

DEATH, NO EXCEPTIONS!

****

Emily finally got up out of bed at approximately 9:15 a.m. She bathed, dressed, fixed her a hot cup of coffee, then started doing a little house cleaning since William was gone.

She figured if she was gonna get something done around the house, now was the time, because as long as William was present, all he wanted her to do was walk around the house with only her bra and a short skirt with no panties on so that he could have sex with her however he wanted to, and wherever he wanted to, inside her house.

She started cleaning out her closet and reorganizing it. While doing so, she gathered all her and Williams' dirty laundry and took them inside her laundry room to get washed. As always, before placing William's clothes into the washer, she checked all his clothes, but this time she mistakenly left four one hundred dollar bills inside the left pocket of her blue jeans. She had determined not to make the same mistake again. Neither with her clothing, nor William's.

As Emily checked through the pockets of William's pants and shorts, she didn't find anything. Therefore, she threw them all into her laundry machine. She was about to throw all of his shirts inside as well, but not before checking one of the shirts that was inside his laundry bag. It was a Khaki all black casual shirt that had two pockets on each side of it, around the upper chest area. Emily checked the pockets and discovered what felt like a neatly folded piece of paper. She unbuttoned the pocket, and retrieved the piece of paper. It was a full-length tablet size piece of paper, which she unfolded out of curiosity. She noticed as she browsed over it, that it looked to be a rough draft letter that William had wrote to someone. When Emily saw the heading "Dear Monica" she figured she had stumbled upon a letter William had written a chick that maybe he was fuckin'. So she stopped everything she was doing and read the letter. What she read caused her to open her mouth in shock and run straight to the telephone to call her friend, Shamika.

Chapter Twenty Seven
[You Gotta Finish What You Started]

Timothy walked out into the prison's parking lot and saw William leaning on the side of his car. As Timothy approached, he started smiling hard. He was happy to see his boy.

"What the fuck up, my nigga?" Timothy greeted, slapping hands with William and giving him a hug.

"Not a muthafuckin' thing, dawg," replied William. They both got into the car. "I'm just glad yo' ass outta that place."

"This is a nice ass ride nigga you got here. You look like yo' ass doing good as a muthafucka!" Timothy spat.

William smiled and then looked over at him, "I'm a'ight. Shit, you remember what you told me right before I left prison, about doing whatchu gotta do while out here?"

"Talking 'bout what I told you as far as get rich or die fucking trying?"

"Yeah," William replied, easing out of the parking lot. "That's exactly what a nigga did, too."

"Shit, William, my nigga, you suppose to."

"But for real, Timothy, I had every muthafucking intention of getting out and getting a job. You know, doing the right thing. But dawg, these crackahs won't let a nigga do the right thing. I tried to get job after job, but these muthafuckas didn't want to take any chances hiring a convicted felon and shit."

"My nigga, I already know how them crackahs play. The system set up for our ass to fail. You dig? The only way a nigga gon' make it out here is to do it the thug way! My nigga, for real, that's all I know," spat Timothy.

"Shit, me, too," replied William, hitting the highway.

"I mean, a nigga took a few classes and shit while doing my damn time. But fuck, you know that's just a part of staying busy while doing time. If a nigga don't stay fucking busy while behind them fucking bars, trapped in that damn cage, his ass'll go fucking crazy!"

"Tell me a fucking bout it," said William, shaking his head. "That's why I vowed on everything not to return to prison again."

"Same here, Will. No bullshit! And, my nigga, I want you to know I appreciate the money you dropped on me."

"That ain't shit, dawg. Told you before I left a nigga had you. I don't bullshit with my word. I know how it is up in that muthafucka."

"Shamika held a nigga down, too. Man, she visited me every damn week and sent me money."

"Dawg, Shamika just like Emily. She's loyal. That's all a nigga need in his corner out here, a loyal, down ass bitch!"

"That's why it doesn't matter if she copped her some dick while I was gone. If she did, her ass was strong enough to not let the dick get in the way of our relationship."

"Right. And, Timothy, dawg, that's all that mattered. 'Cause shit, when a bitch let a nigga get her pussy, mind and heart, that's when a nigga in prison got trouble on his damn hands."

"Nah, William. That's when a nigga in prison need to say fuck that stankin' ass bitch and let her go!'

"My point exactly," replied William. "My point exactly. But look, beside all of that, open that glove compartment and grab that lil brown paper bag."

Timothy did as William requested of him. "That's yours, my nigga," William said.

"Timothy took a peep into the bag, "Damn," he spat, seeing nothing but cash.

"How much is it, William?"

"Five g's. And, you see that bag down by your foot?"

"Yeah," replied Timothy.

"In it is two fresh ass Karl Kani outfits. I know you like that casual shit. One outfit is black. The other is all white. A nigga brought you two pair of suede and leather Ballys to match your outfits. I remember you telling me how much you love them Ballys."

"Damn, dawg, I appreciate this. I swear I do. How did you know my size though?"

"Hell, beside you and I being the same damn height and size for real, I called Shamika from my Auntie Pearl's house and she told me everything I needed to know. But dawg, Shamika was mad as a muthafucka that I was coming to pick you up and not her."

"She was, huh?"

"Damn right. You know that girl love the hell out of you."

"I know. And I love her, too, but it's business before pleasure. So tell me, my nigga, are you out here or what? You know, in this dope game? I mean, you hit a nigga off pretty good, you know."

"Timothy, a nigga stung this bitch for three kilos and a lot of cash."

"Say whut?"

"Damn right. It was costly though. I had to cut her son's finger off, 'cause the bitch tried to play me. When she saw my ass was serious, she took the cotton outta her fucking mouth and told me everything."

"So how did you find out about this chick? Was she somebody you were fuckin'? 'Cause yo ass love them bitches."

William started laughing. "Nah, I wasn't fucking her. I was fucking her friend though. That's who hipped me to her. The bitch ended up killing her friend later on."

"Damn," spat Timothy. "The bitch vicious like that?"

"She had the ups is all I can tell you. She meant to kill me, too, but I'm still here."

"So the bitch still in Charlotte, William?"

"More than likely."

"Dawg, you gotta finish what you started. The bitch tried to kill you. We got to see her ass about that, my nigga."

"That's the thing, Timothy, I let the matter go. Even sent the bitch a letter and everything."

"What made you do that, William?"

"What?"

"Write the bitch a letter, seeing that the bitch tried to take your life and shit?"

"I just didn't want any further blood shed, you feel me? I mean, yeah, the bitch tried to take my life, but shit, she had her reasons. I cut her son's finger off and took her shit.

Who wouldn't have wanted to get a nigga for that?"

"I can understand all of that. But what I can't understand is you letting this bitch slide after her attempt to take you out had failed. And for real, my nigga, you don't even have to go into it deep with me. The only thing that really matters is you're alive and well. But William, we got to get this chick."

"Like I said, dawg, I thought long and hard on that shit. Before I sent the letter to her ass, I laid in the cut on her. I spotted her with her son, and two other niggas.

The bitch didn't even have any idea that I was watching her with the intent of putting a bullet in her fucking brain. I considered this though, Timothy—"

"What's that?" Timothy said, cutting him off.

"I considered the fact that the bitch didn't get her coke back; she didn't get any of her money back; and neither did she succeed in her attempt to kill me. I knew where I could find her ass, but she didn't have a clue as to where she could find me. I took all of this into consideration along with the fact that I was just thankful to God for still being alive. Thinking hard on those things made me say, fuck it! Taking her life isn't worth it!

The whole while William was talking, Timothy was pulling hairs from his goatee.

"William, my nigga, I hear what you are saying, and I ain't the one to say whether you handled the matter after that bitch tried to take you out, right or not. I just want you to know that yo' nigga's home now. And

I ain't even gon' bullshit around with you. All while I was doing my time, all I could think about was getting out and making money.

I'm out now, my nigga, and money is on my mind. My motto is still GET RICH, OR DIE TRYING! I'm sure you all about the same," he said, looking over at William.

"Most definitely, nigga," William replied.

"The thing is, we don't need to be watching our back every damn where we go. That's why I believe this bitch that you robbed is a problem that we must solve. Especially since we gon' be doing our thing in the Queen City."

"Shit, to be honest with you, I had talked to Emily about moving up out of the Queen City. Her ass don't wanna do that though."

"Shit, William, do you blame her? Like you and I, the girl was born in the muthafucka."

"I know," replied William. "But dawg, sometimes you gotta change your environment if you plan on changing your ways."

"Who the fuck trying to change? I know I'm not. Are you? Shit, I'm a thug for life!"

William slowly shook his head in the negative. He briefly reflected on his life. His auntie Annie Pearl had adopted him because his own damn parents were so caught up in their own little world of negativity that they couldn't provide a decent future for him. In spite of his auntie Annie Pearl doing her best to raise him up the right way in the church, with a focus on treating others how he would want others to treat him, still he drifted into the the streets and started thuggin'. Thuggin' landed his ass in the State Penal System, where he was determined to get his life on track, but he realized that life's highway isn't always a smooth road to travel; that some things won't always go as you plan or intend for them to go, because there are many potholes and bumps in the road despite your good intention to do this, or that.

Falling in some potholes on this road called life, and having a near death experience was enough truthfully to at least cause him to think about giving change a try. But how could he tell this to Timothy? He knew from doing prison time with Timothy that he was a real nigga. He was in prison for nearly shooting a man to death for looking at his girl, Shamika, the wrong way. That's why Shamika stuck by his side the whole time he was in prison. He was charged and convicted of assault with intent to kill with a dangerous weapon. He didn't plan on returning.

Timothy loved guns and doing things the thug way. William finally snapped out of his reflecting over his life and said, "Timothy, ain't nothing wrong with changing."

"I didn't say that there was. All I said was I ain't trying to change, are you?"

"All I'm trying to do is take one day at a time, my nigga. It's cold out here in this world."

"That's why I plan on wrapping up real tight. Now man, what we gon' do? Cause for real, I don't have any kids. I'm thirty-one years old, and my parents are in the damn military stationed somewhere over in Germany. All I got is my boo Shamika and you, my number one muthafuckin' nigga. And if we are going to be getting muthafuckin' money in the Queen City, we don't need that bitch you robbed or anyone associated with her looking for you. And trust me, if you cut that bitch son's finger off, and she knows that you are still alive even after her attempt to kill you, then hey, you do the math."

"Okay, so shit, Timothy, what you think should be done?"

"The bitch gotta go in the dirt. Simple as that! And my nigga since you have kept it real with me, I'll bury the bitch myself. All you gotta do is show me where she live."

"You'll drop that bitch just like that, huh, nigga?"

"Goddamn right! You never start something without finishing it. Not out here in the streets, William. Fuck nah! It's the thug way or the highway! Fuck that other bullshit!"

"You got a point," replied William. "You definitely got a point."

"I know I do. I been in the streets all my damn life pretty much. The only mistake I see you made from dealing with this bitch was sending her ass that letter."

"Damn, why you say that dawg?"

"Cause the bitch thought she killed you. But when she received that letter from you, she realized for certain that she didn't. Now, her mistake with you was, her ass should have doubled checked to see if you were dead. She slipped big time by not doing that. Little mistakes like that can be costly. That's why when we see this bitch again, it's gonna be lights out, party over, my nigga. Trust me, I got this!"

****

"You ain't gonna believe this shit here, Shamika," spat Emily with the phone to her ear.

"Okay, Emily, what is it now?"

"Girl first of all, you were absolutely right as hell about what you said to me yesterday."

"Emily I said a lot yesterday. What did I say that got yo' white ass so hyper today"?

"Remember you told me what is done in the dark will eventually come to light."

"Yeah I did." Shamika said biting her lip.

"I found this letter in Williams' shirt pocket. At first, I didn't think nothing of it but when I saw Dear Monica, I thought this was some chick he was cheating on my ass with."

"Well, was he?"

"Hell nah! It's worst. The content of the letter said the chick was a drug dealer that his ass robbed!"

"What!"

"Damn right, girl. And guess what?" Emily summarized the letter. His ass cut the chick's child's finger off, girl."

"Nah girl, that nigga ain't that crazy, is he?"

Emily read the letter to her.

"I got to see that damn letter, cause if that nigga did that shit to a child, his ass got problems."

Emily was so shocked upon finding the letter in Williams's pocket. She finished reading the letter to her girl, Shamika. Her hands were shaking from finding out this information.

"What else it say?"

"That ain't all though. The chick shot and killed her best fuckin' friend.

William mentioned in the letter that her killing her friend wasn't justifiable. Shamika, you and I know damn near everybody in damn Queen City. We got to find out who this Monica is."

"We sho' do, girl. That's why I'm on my way over to your place right damn now," said Shamika.

"Well, you know William went to go pick up Timothy. And they probably will be pulling up shortly. So—"

"That don't even matter right now. Just keep that letter on the low-low 'til I get there.

You and I are about to do some investigating of our own."

"That's a bet, girl. I'll see you when you get here."

Emily disconnected her and Shamika's conversation. She then folded the letter up and put it in her pocket. *I fuckin' knew this muthafucka was hiding something from me. I fuckin' knew it!*

[Stay Tuned For Death, No Exceptions 2]

Readers' Guide

Do you believe that Monica should have been straight forward with Williams (the robber) when he demanded her to tell him where she was keeping her coke and cash?

Do you believe that Williams cutting Monica's son (Ali) finger off was necessary? What do you think Monica could have done to prevent William from cutting her son's finger off?

Do you believe the death of Yolanda who was Monica's best friend was necessary or even justifiable? If yes, or no – why?

Do you believe that Monica's attempt to kill William was necessary? Why?

What do you believe should have been Ricky and Bootsy's response to not only Monica getting robbed, but her son's finger getting cutting off? What should have been their response to Monica killing Yolanda who was like family to them all?

As a mother of a young son, do you believe Monica should have even been involved in dealing drugs?

How do you feel the tragedy of little Ali getting his finger cut off will affect him in the future?

If you answered any of these questions, please be advised that there is no right, or wrong answers. Your answers to the questions are your OPINION. With that, your opinion is very much appreciated.

I want to thank you for purchasing and reading this book. It is my great hope that by having this book in your possession and answering these questions, I will receive the inspiration needed to bring forth the Sequel to Death, No Exceptions!

DEATH, NO EXCEPTIONS!

Please enjoy the first two chapters of my next novella, Father Forgive Me, which will be released in 2009. Holler at me and may the Creator smile on you with His blessings everyday of your life!

Sincerely Yours,
Kareem
Kareem Tomblin #10119-058
Federal Correction Center
Post Office Box 52020/Unit B-2
Bennettsville, SC 29512

Bio
Kareem Tomblin

Kareem Tomblin, a.k.a., "Soojah" is currently incarcerated in a federal correction institution, located in Bennesville, South Carolina. He has been incarcerated since 1992. He has never allowed his present confinement to stop him from accomplishing his dreams of bringing the ghetto gospel of truth to those who have eyes to read and ears to hear. Kareem lets readers know, in his first street story that the warning he is ultimately delivering is simple, whatever decision one chooses to make in life do it with wise direction. Because in this world of sin, motivated by dividends, one slip, or wrong turn could lead to Death, No Exceptions! Bottom Line.

Father, Forgive Me
Synopsis

Whether in prison, or out in the so-called free world, when a man sees a woman whom he deems uncompromisingly worthy of pursuing, it would take a nation of millions to hold him back from having her. Federal inmate, Korey Taylor was of no exception. He was young, good-looking, full of testosterone and God-fearing.

When Korey laid eyes on a Federal Bureau of Prisons employee, who not only worked for the government, but was also another man's property, he found himself faced with strong sexual urges for her and a determination to fulfill them. All at the expense of inadvertently embracing what is morally wrong, in spite of having sufficient Biblical knowledge of what's morally right.

Follow Korey Taylor as he takes us on a lustful ride through his head as he attempts to please his flesh until unexpected events leave him pleading to God for forgiveness.

Chapter One
More Than I Desired to Say No To

The teaching of the Holy Bible records in no uncertain terms, that all have sinned and come short of the glory of God. I was of no exception. I had issues. Being incarcerated since my late teens, with more time on my hands to serve than a Rolex watch, was one issue. I was faced with the reality of leaving prison an old ass man—a reality I definitely refused to accept. Therefore, I stayed my ass in the Law Library, fighting my case.

However, I had another issue which was continuously wandering in the wilderness of lustful thoughts while here in prison. My lustful thoughts weren't just any o' lustful thoughts. Like lusting for a big house on a hill, or lusting for a nice automobile, or even lusting for an extremely large bank account. My lustful thoughts were for a woman, but not just any woman. I'm talking about a woman who was already another man's property. Damn right, the chick had already walked down that aisle and said, *I Do*. Who the hell was I to keep thinking about fucking her like she belonged to me, and only me!?

I was beating my meat on this chick three to four times a day, as if my problem was that of a nympho! Beating your meat as those of us who are incarcerated call it, meant that you were masturbating! I was certainly no stranger to it. But fuck it, what else was I to do when I thought about this chick and felt horny—pray? Well, I tried that and discovered on many occasions while on my knees that I would have to stop praying, because my mind would become bombarded with thoughts of this chick, clouding what I wanted to focus on saying in my prayer.

Besides, I definitely wasn't gonna stoop to the low-level of fucking a man, as many male prisoners were doing. Shit, grant it, I was a freak, but I was also a believer in God, my Heavenly Father. I read His word, the Holy Bible, all the time. I knew exactly what it had to say concerning men having sex with other men. It was an abomination! Meaning, such an act was extremely disgusting in the sight of God (Leviticus 18:6), so I wasn't going that route.

Although I wasn't into fucking another man up his ass like it was a woman's pussy, or allowing another man to suck my dick, I was committing the act of adultery all the same—in my head—by wanting so badly to fuck, the freak out of another man's woman. I knew that according to the Old Testament of the Holy Bible, this act was also forbidden by God, and if two were caught committing such an act, death would be their reward (John 8:3-5).

Committing such an act was serious, even if I was committing it mentally. But I was fucking hardheaded, in spite of what I knew. All my life I had been like that. I sold drugs when the law said that it was illegal to do so. I carried guns when the law revealed that to do so, one had to have a permit. Even before those incidents, I was a hardheaded youth.

My mother would set a curfew for me to be inside the house on school nights by seven p.m. But guess the fuck what? I would bring my ass in at eight, or maybe nine. Now, many years later, here I was in prison still being hardheaded, fucking someone else's wife in my head. Every time I saw this chick, I was breaking God's law—committing adultery. Whether I saw her from afar, close up, or just plain out in my damn mind, lust for her was being conceived. And you know what? It was more than I desired to say no to.

Chapter Two
Mrs. Asia Martin

Keeping it real, this sistah had me wondering like I was lost in unfamiliar territory. I wanted to know everything about her, even her Zodiac sign. Was it Aries, Leo, or Sagittarius? All of which were FIRE signs. I definitely was burning inside from the flaming fire that kept coming over me, especially whenever I would be directly in her presence.

Asia Martin was my case manager while I was serving time in a United States Penitentiary (USP) located in Allenwood, Pennsylvania. Allenwood was a maximum security prison. The kind where the government sent people like mob bosses, corrupt CIA officials, big drug dealers, and the like. I was sent to this muthafuckin' place by the government at the age of nineteen years old, for allegedly being a member and active participant of a crew the prosecuting attorneys for the government of the Western District of North Carolina, Charlotte referred to as The Bang Bang Gang!

According to the government, The Bang Bang Gang (BBG) was responsible for numerous home invasions of rival drug dealers, as well as robberies of the same rival drug dealers, and countless violent shootings. The prosecuting attorneys claimed that BBG was so notorious in the city of Charlotte, that nearly every weapon in the federal arsenal was used to remove us from free society.

I was the juvenile of this alleged crew. But instead of sending my so-called gangsta ass to a juvenile facility, after all was said and done with my trial proceedings, I was sent to USP in Atlanta, then transferred to USP in Allenwood, all in an effort to treat me as an adult defendant.

I stayed in Allenwood seven years. Mrs. Asia Martin was assigned to my case, the last three years I spent in Allenwood. She had just gotten there from the Lewisburg penitentiary. Her transfer was a promotion. When I first laid eyes on her, I noticed she didn't have the facial features of a Halle Berry, or a Stacey Dash. In comparison to either of those beauties, she wouldn't have stood a chance from the neck up. Not that sistah wasn't a cutie, indeed to me she was. It's just that she wasn't one of those pretty red model type chicks.

She was as dark as the oil in the Middle East. But to me that was her badge of sexiness and true physical beauty. Every since I can remember, I have always been deeply attracted to sistahs who had the skin tone of my African ancestors. No offense to light skinned chicks, or even white chicks, because it's a fact that many of them are beautiful and very sexy. However, it was sistah dark skin who was my type of hype.

Mrs. Asia Martin was also slightly bowlegged, five-six in height and weighed maybe 165 pounds. And all of her weight was in the right spots—her ass and thighs! She didn't wear nothing but dresses and stiletto heels to match, with a sexy ass feminine swagger to compliment her dress code. Mrs. Asia Martin's hair, which was so long it reached the top of her buttocks, was in nice thin-like dreadlocks. She always had them pulled back into a ponytail. Whenever I would be in her presence, I would notice that her dreadlocks didn't smell like piss. A lot of people assumed that dreadlocks smelled horrible and they spread the rumor like wild fire. But Mrs. Asia Martin's dreadlocks had the aroma of a fruity strawberry perfume or oil, which always was pleasing to my sensitive nostrils.

One evening while in Mrs. Asia Martin's office, after a program review, I asked her out of sheer curiosity about her dreads. I said, "Mrs. Asia, (she didn't mind being addressed by her first name) what made you decide to grow your hair long and in dreadlocks?" Sistah wasted no time answering me. She looked me squarely in my hazel green eyes with her big pretty dark brown eyes, her eyebrows arched thin and sexy and replied, "I got my hair this way because I like keeping things natural."

Mrs. Asia's voice was soft and sweet. Upon hearing it and her making eye contact with me, my dick literally started rising like the morning sun. I was thinking to myself, *What could be more natural than me closing your office door, lifting your dress up, ripping your panties off, laying you down on the carpet of your office floor, putting your legs on top of my shoulders and fucking you till you tell me to stop?*

Mrs. Asia must've saw my eyes weaken while that dirty ass thought was going through my head, because she said, "Korey Taylor, are you alright?" Then she walked over to a table in her office to make coffee. Before I could even reply, I noticed my hard-on was showing through my light-gray sweat pants. I tried to cover it with the oversized 2X white T-shirt that I was wearing, but to no avail. My hard-on could still be seen poking out.

I turned sideways, and replied, "Yes, ma'am, I'm alright." I lied. Shit, the truth is, I was burning the fuck up, wanting to put my dick in her.When Mrs. Asia finished drinking her coffee, she walked back over to her desk to sit down. My eyes were stuck on her soft-looking ass the whole time. That muthafuckah was shaking like an individual with Parkinson Disease! I wanted to bite her ass so bad like it was a damn hamburger from McDonalds. It looked so good to me. With sistah's ass shaking like it was, I knew she couldn't have been wearing regular panties, which made me conclude, she had to be wearing a thong! Such a sight and thought didn't ease my hard-on any. Instead, it worsened. My dick was so hard; I could feel the muthafuckah pulsating!

When Mrs. Asia finally sat that nice juicy ass of hers down, I was left standing sideways. I was about to exit her office to avoid embarrassment, but sistah stopped me.

She said, "Before you leave, Korey Taylor, I need you to sign your progress report."

When she said that I initially thought, Ah fuck! My ass going to solitary confinement today because the very first thing Mrs. Asia gonna see when I walk toward her is my hard-on and she gonna perceive my ass to be a muthafuckin' pervert! There is no way she's gonna miss it, or forgive me for it. I didn't want to end up in solitary confinement for being perceived as a pervert. But what the fuck, I conceded. I wasn't a fake ass negro, either. Shit, I was human. And, if nothing else, it was showing.

I reluctantly walked over to Mrs. Asia's desk. Thankfully, she had her head down while I walked toward her. Sistah was looking down at the paperwork that she wanted me to sign. I got to her desk and quickly bent over with my elbows on her desk. I signed the paperwork, purposely taking my time in the process. I was hoping that by me taking my time, my hard-on would subside before I stood back up. But guess what? My fucking hoping didn't produce any fruit. Because when I finished signing the papers she wanted me to sign, even after taking my time, I could still feel my hard-on at its peak, throbbing. Now I know you're probably saying, "Damn, Negro what the fuck was you on, Viagra?!"

Nope, it was just bottled up lust that made my dick solid hard for Mrs. Asia's goods. I went on ahead and stood myself up. When I did, she looked up at me. I was so close to her desk that when she looked up, my hard dick was right at her face where her mouth is. Had she leaned forward an inch, my dick would have touched the ruby red lipstick she had on. What made matters worse was I didn't wear those tight ass underwear that hugged a man's balls and suppressed his dick when it was inflated and rock hard. I wore loose boxer shorts, the kind that gave your dick the freedom to come forth unhindered. This day, though, I wished that reality wasn't so for the sake of me avoiding being embarrassed.

When Mrs. Asia saw my dick pointed outward toward her mouth, she eased her head back looking up at me, as if to say, *No, the brutha didn't!* Sistah stood up fast with what appeared to me an angry attitude, strangely mixed with a bit of sympathy for my young ass.

She said with her eyebrows folded, "Korey Taylor, I see you're having a hard time..."

I immediately cut her off in my thoughts and said to myself, "Damn right, I'm having a hard time, Miss Sexy Ass! And you can make it easier for me if you take it out of my sweat pants and start sucking it."

I snapped my ass back to reality and replied, "Mrs. Asia, please forgive me. I'm sorry, I didn't mean any offense. I'm just sensitive..."

I wasn't the type of person who would just outright disrespect any woman. My mother was a woman. Plus, I had two beautiful sisters. I loved both my mother and my sisters to death. I wouldn't dare want a guy disrespecting either of them, under any circumstances. So, it was my belief and duty to carry myself respectfully with a woman, just as I would want a guy to be with my mother and sisters.

I don't know how in the hell I got myself caught up in wanting Mrs. Asia so damn bad that I would literally spend countless minutes and hours solid rock hard wanting to fuck her. Sistah walked over to her shredder machine and shredded a few sheets of paper.

She then said to me, "You don't have to explain yourself to me. I know you're human, and I know where you're at. Just try to contain your sensitivity a little better."

When sistah said that, I thought to myself, How in the hell you expect a young healthy ass man like me to contain himself in your presence when you're bouncing your booty around this office of yours, like it's a basketball?! I came back to reality without trippin' and replied saying, "Yes, ma'am, I'll do the best I can."

Mrs. Asia had just spared my ass a first class ticket to solitary confinement. And trust me sistah wasn't the type to spare a brutha for being what she considered disrespectful. Mrs. Asia would lock a brutha up for something as simple as looking at her ass too hard while she's on the prison compound, walking from this location to that location.

I witnessed her do it before. She locked two guys' asses up for looking at her ass one day while she was leaving one of the prison's housing units. So, I knew sistah didn't play. Yet she spared me and I was standing in front of her with my dick aiming at her mouth. I thought on this a few minutes, before she interrupted and said, "I'll have a copy of your progress report to give you on tomorrow. You can come pick it up at around six o'clock."

Other Book From Prioritybooks Publishing

Sex on the 2nd Floor
Or anywhere else you can get it!

    Jessica Williamson never dreamed that the fire in her would unleash an insurmountable passion when she hired the sexy and handsome Travis Ingram to maintain the company's computer system. Not only did he capture her heart but his mere presence caused havoc, backstabbing, confusion and sexual tension at the office. Jessica finds herself changing from upstanding and happily married to an oversexed, overheated, and hot between the legs adulteress. Will Jessica and Travis control the passion that threatens to destroy everything they worked so hard to obtain? Or will they succumb to the passion in their hearts? Jazz Catrell weaves an interesting tale of love in the workplace and how listening to your heart is not always the right thing to do.

Distributors: Ingram, Baker and Taylor & Lushena
Amazon.com, Barnes & Noble.com
www.sex-on-the-second-floor.blogspot.com

Email: jazzcatrell@yahoo.com
ISBN: 978-0-9753634-8-5
$14.95

STILL GHETTO
The Sequel
By Mary L. Wilson

Mary L. Wilson, Queen of the Ink Pen, returns with the highly anticipated sequel to Ghetto Luv. Join Mya and Libra once again as they battle against deception, destruction and death in the drama-filled streets of the Lou. Brazen and bold, the mistress of seduction is back and she is sexier than ever. With a major record deal, a handsome husband and a precious son, life couldn't be any better. But problems and trouble lingers near. The twists and turns that occur in this tangled tale will leave readers begging for more.

ISBN: 978-09792823-6-2
http://www.prioritybooks.com

$14.95

Ghetto Luv
Urban novel takes you straight to the 'hood and leaves you laughing

Sassy. Urban. Funny. Mary Wilson's *Ghetto Luv* is "in your face," with the cat-and-mouse game between the Keke and Libra as the backdrop. Keke is one of the most handsome brothas in the 'hood, definitely smooth when it comes to the ladies.

Neighborhood diva Libra is described as "every man's dream and every woman's nightmare." She and her two girls rule the streets, but Libra is clearly the standout of the three. She is full of spunk, confidence and street smarts - the mistress of seduction with her drop-dead gorgeous looks. Looking for the queen of St. Louis' West End? Libra holds the title and the attitude to go along with it.

The novel is soaked with brazen sex and hardcore violence. You'll understand why when you meet Libra's girlfriends.

Books can be purchased at most on-line stores such as Amazon and Barnes and Noble. Books are distributed by Ingram. Contact the author at MaryLWilson2003@yahoo.com Or visit her at www.myspace.com/msghettoluv

P R I C E L E S S
BY ANN CLAY

Keisha McKenzie-Logan, a young professional, happy in her singleness, and passionate about her community finds herself caught up by standards she and her peers have decided would be the ideal mate for someone of her stature. However, when she finds herself smitten by the likes of the handsome security guard, Wendell Russell, her crusade to resist him becomes a battle she ultimately loses when she learns that everything is not always what it seems.

ISBN: 978-0979282393
http://www.prioritybooks.com

$11.95

DESTRUCTION VIA THE MIRROR IMAGE
BY STANLEY PITCHFORD

Stanley Pitchford's book is about twelve astronauts picked to explore outer space in hopes of finding a discovery interesting to mankind. Once in space, they encounter a creature on the ship. This creature is so hard to figure out that they must find the monster's weakness in order to destroy it. On this space exploration, lives are sacrificed, passion and romance erupts while blackmail attempts surface. Author Stanley Pitchford weaves an interesting and unique science fiction novel that explores outer space and shows what can happen when we attempt to address the unknown universe.

ISBN:978-0979282379
http://www.prioritybooks.com

$14.95

FINDING FOREVER
BY KEISHA ERVIN

Keisha Ervin returns with her first novella. *Finding Forever* is filled with drama, love, disloyalty, and hope for the future.

It is said that if you let something go and it returns, it was always yours to begin with. Does true love really exist? For Koran, it did more than eight years ago when the love of his life left without an explanation. Once brokenhearted, time heals all things and being the big baller that he is, love for him now is riding around in his expensive cars, wearing the best jewelry money can buy and staying dipped in the latest fashions, while lying back in his beautiful crib.

ISBN: 978-0-9816483-4-7
http://www.prioritybooks.com

$14.95

Simply Put!
"A message to young brothers in the "free world" and those incarcerated!"

By Kareem Tomblin

PriorityBooks Current Books Order Form

Indicate the number of copies of each book you wish to purchase then click the calculate button for Total.

Book Title	Copies	Price	Total
Sumthin' T' Say		$14.95	
Ghetto Luv		$14.95	
Sex on the Second Floor		$14.95	
Lovers' Anonymous		$14.95	
Destruction Via the Mirror		$14.95	
Priceless		$11.95	
Still Ghetto		$14.95	
Simply Put!		$9.00	
		Sub-Total:	
Shipping & Handling ($3.95 per book):			
		Total:	